Two hearts collide . . .

Zoey Appleton, whose idyllic young life is shattered by the most senseless of tragedies, but whose passionate heart never dies. **Tristan March**, raised in the wilds of Alaska and the paradise of Hawaii, a thrill-seeker who finds beauty in every woman, but has never, ever believed in true love.

. . . at University Hospital

University

HOSPITAL

Condition Critical

CHERIE BENNETT
and JEFF GOTTESFELD

BERKLEY JAM BOOKS, NEW YORK

This is a work of fiction. Names, characters, places, and incidents are either the product of the authors' imaginations or are used fictitiously, and any resemblance to actual persons, living or dead, business establishments, events or locales is entirely coincidental.

UNIVERSITY HOSPITAL: CONDITION CRITICAL

A Berkley Jam book / published by arrangement with the authors

PRINTING HISTORY
Berkley Jam edition / December 1999

The Penguin Putnam Inc. World Wide Web site address is
http://www.penguinputnam.com

ISBN: 0-425-17256-2

BERKLEY JAM BOOKS®
Berkley Jam Books are published by The Berkley Publishing Group,
a division of Penguin Putnam Inc.,
375 Hudson Street, New York, New York 10014.
BERKLEY JAM and its logo
are trademarks belonging to Penguin Putnam Inc.

PRINTED IN THE UNITED STATES OF AMERICA

10 9 8 7 6 5 4 3 2 1

For Kat

University
HOSPITAL

Condition Critical

1

TRISTAN

We're in the secret room.

Fable Harbor University Hospital. Fifth floor of the old wing. Supposedly closed for renovation. Third room on the right.

Contents? Two metal hospital beds with no railings. Five standard-issue orange plastic cafeteria chairs. Three puke-brown Formica nightstands. Six hanging sick-white-light overhead fluorescents.

And us.

Becky Silver, Chad Rourke, and me. Three fresh-out-of-high-schoolers chosen for this rarefied summer-before-college medical program called SCRUBS.

In theory, we're red hots.

In reality, we rank lower than janitorial scum.

The other two SCRUBS, Summer Everly and Zoey Appleton, are elsewhere at the moment. But with Becky and Chad and me are two not-so-patient

FHUH patients, Rick and Shane Carr, identical in looks but not in spirit, age eighteen, currently awaiting heart-lung transplants or death, whichever comes first.

On-the-verge-of-death Rick has fallen madly, passionately, et cetera, for not-likely-to-die-anytime-soon SCRUB Becky. She loves him, too. It's poetic, I suppose. But utterly foreign to me.

Rick is how we got in here. He is the possessor of The Key. Which fits into The Lock. Which locks the door to The Secret Room that Tia built. Against all rules, risking her own job, Tia gave Rick The Key. For him and Becky. For privacy. For love.

Nurse Tia Seng. Beautiful. Smart. Fierce. Tender. Dead.

Three days ago I watched Tia get crushed to death. I've dealt with worse. Life and death are cheap in northern Alaska. But that doesn't make this hurt any less.

I wasn't alone. The other SCRUBS, another nurse, and a bunch of pediatrics patients already looking death in the face stood by helplessly as the whole thing happened.

Me. Tia. And sunny six-year-old Kelly Markell, who has brittle diabetes. All three of us pinned beneath twisted metal. Tia dies, Kelly lives. Which is, come to think of it, the way that Tia would have wanted it.

We're here in The Secret Room for a personal memorial. We come to praise Tia, not to bury her.

She already got buried earlier today. So we drink red Gallo out of the little Dixie cups that don't hold more than a person can spit, which you always find in hospital rooms.

Becky mentions she left Zoey a note, telling her where we are. So she could join us.

Zoey. Zee. The maddening one. She irritates and intrigues. I don't know if I can face her just yet.

As for Summer's whereabouts, who knows? Summer is, like her namesake, elemental. Comes and goes like the clouds. By night, in my arms, she's perfumed vapor. By day, roaming the hallowed healing halls of FHUH, she's ice.

Vapor. Ice. Zee is never, ever either. She tries, fails, flounders, tries to hide it, fails, and I want to wrap her in my arms.

Zoey. Summer. Me. Life.

It sure beats the alternative. Right, Tia? Because your funeral was deeply depressing.

"If my parents poured this swill in their bar in Chicago," my roommate Chad says, "they'd go out of business in about two days." He sips his Dixie and makes a face.

Becky downs hers. She's lying next to Rick on one of the beds. His arms hold her many curves, their hands intertwined.

"I thought you didn't drink," Becky tells Chad.

Shane, Rick's twin, sits in a wheelchair and scowls at his brother and Becky.

They are too blissed to notice.

I do notice.

"I don't drink," Chad admits. "But for Tia, I'm making an exception." He downs the Dixie.

I lift my cup to the fluorescents. "Here's to exceptions."

We all raise our Dixies, even Shane. A chorus of hear-hears. I tilt my head back and pour. It's rot-gut but divine, because I am alive.

"More?" Becky asks me.

"Why not?"

The door opens. It's Zoey. Dressed, of course, maddeningly Zee, in faded jeans, untied canvas sneakers, black sweatshirt, a messy ponytail. The curve of the exposed back of her neck fills me with tenderness.

Becky's golden face lights up when Zoey enters, and even her wild dark curls seem to grin at the presence of her new-best-friend.

"Where were you?" Becky asks. "I'm outnumbered by strong young men."

All enigmatic Zoey says is "Hey."

I study Zee. Her lower lip quivers slightly, like she's biting it on the inside. Her eyes bottomless. I know that look. I've *had* that look.

She's seen a ghost in the past minute.

I scan the room to see if anyone else picks it up. No. People are so oblivious.

But who is Zee's ghost? Tia? Her parents? Some kid who coded on her way up here?

Who?

Zee's trying to hide it, playing normal, but she can't hide it from me.

My mind presses Rewind and it's back four hours. We're all at the Sengs' house, after the funeral, at Tia's wake. I can't stand the suffocating crush indoors. So I take a walk around the house.

And there she is.

Zee has slipped into the backyard. Her head is tilted to the slate gray sky. In conversation with God? With the sky? With herself?

She feels my presence. Shares with me and the slate gray sky a secret. In return, I tell her nothing. I never do. Then she's crying. I hold her. Supposedly, I am comforting her. Really I am comforting myself for comforting her, for being too whatever and whomever I am to share my secrets with anyone.

Ever.

As Zoey cries in grief, I find myself focusing on the glow of her hair, the sinews and velvet of her skin, the feel of quintessential Zee, and I want to . . .

God. I am the world's biggest schmuck. Brass hole. Zee speak, for cursing without cursing. Even that quirk of hers is under my skin.

Zoey catches me watching her. I raise my eyebrows. Who's the ghost, Zee?

"We were just about to start telling Tia stories," Chad tells Zoey, and she yanks her eyes away from me. "That's what you do at an Irish wake, anyway."

Zee hides her ghost under the bed and smiles. "So I've heard."

"Want some wine?" Shane offers.

"Red wine is good for your heart," Rick adds.

The brothers find this hilarious. Becky punches Rick playfully as Chad tosses Zoey a Dixie. She catches it behind her back, Shane fills it, and she drops into orange plastic. But Zoey never drinks. So what's she going to do?

"So, Tia stories. Who's first?" Rick asks.

Chad, still suffering from Chicago Catholic parochial schoolboy disease, raises his hand. When no one calls on him, he proceeds anyway. "What I'll never forget is Tia trying to scoop the vodka out of the punch at Leo's party. After it had been in there a while."

"What I'll never, ever forget," Becky says, "is being on the peds floor and hearing the shelves crash in the closet. I go running to the supply closet and tear the door open, thinking some kid has fainted or died in there or something, and there's Tia and Marcus, macking away, totally oblivious."

We all laugh. Even Zee, though in her eyes I see that the ghost has crept back out from under the bed.

"What I'll never forget," Shane says, for once not scowling, "is how she was with Leo. When her baby bro screwed up on the ward, she busted his chops like nobody's business. But if anyone else tried to bust him, Tia was like a pit bull."

Agreement murmuring all around.

"She was nice," I say. "When we got here. More than anyone else at this hospital, she was nice."

"Oh?" Chad asks mockingly, slightly buzzed as the Gallo takes hold way down South in Dixie. "You wouldn't have wanted to trade her in for The Virus?"

Becky shudders dramatically and holds her throat, and we laugh. The Virus, Dr. Vivian Pace, Associate Administrator of FHUH. Our boss. She's the beauty and the damned. She loathes us.

"You know that reeper, Zelda, the lady with the crazy wigs?" Zoey asks, contemplating her untouched cup of Gallo. "The one in and out of the ER? Zelda can hardly remember her own name, but she knows all the words to all these old songs. Tia used to sing with her. Everyone else ran away. But Tia sat there, so patiently. And sang."

The silence is deafening. Zoey is telling the truth. We all run from Zelda.

"I'd say this calls for a toast," Mr. Nice Guy Chad proclaims, to fill the sad silence. "When you're the son of bar owners, you've got a sixth sense for these things."

Instantly the Dixie cups are filled all around. Except Zee's, which is still full.

"To Tia," Chad toasts.

"To Tia," we echo. Bottoms up.

Damn. She drank it.

Zoey puts down her empty Dixie, and her eyes meet mine. I see the ghost. She looks away. But she can feel me, knows I know. I know it.

"See, this is why you gotta do what you want to do when you want to do it." Chad is rolling now, his words a little slurred. " 'Cuz you never know, man."

"Tell that to yourself," I advise him.

He points at me. "You're right. Totally right. I'm givin' Eve that letter tomorrow. Tomorrow. 'Cuz I love her, man."

I know what he's referring to, but everyone else is clueless. Chad can share when and if the spirit moves him. Because I'm not talking.

"And I love *her*, man," Rick declares, nuzzling Becky's neck.

"That right?" Shane muses, an edge to his voice. "Get it while you can, bro', 'cuz you could be chomping worms this time next week."

"Don't say that," Becky snaps.

"We all gotta go sometime, man," Chad says, waxing drunkenly philosophical.

"Some of us sooner than others," Shane adds, with the bite of a guy who could die any day from secondary cardiopulmonary hypertension.

"That kind of negativity doesn't help anyone," Becky tells him as her arms tighten protectively around his mirror image.

"You miss my point," Shane explains. "I'm looking forward to that day."

Rick insists that his brother, Shane, doesn't mean it. Shane insists that he does, too.

"Well, you're gonna be the loser then, bro," Rick says, feigning nonchalance. " 'Cuz you're gonna live. I'm kinda set on having you around."

Silence.

Everyone surely thinking what I'm thinking: Rick coded not so long ago. We held a vigil outside his room with the kids in the peds ward. Rick lived. But barely. Everyone's praying a tissue-matching heart-lung donor will come along before he codes again. Genetically, he and Shane are the same. So if and when compatible organs come available, a transplant could save either of them.

But only one of them.

Who to save? They agreed long ago to decide it by a coin toss.

Shane scratches his cheek, eyes his brother. The darkness in his eyes has gone twinkly. "Well, who cares if you want me around? 'Cuz everyone knows, man, you're a butthole."

And then the family musical begins.

"You look like a butt hole . . ." the twins sing, holding the "oh" in butt hole so long that I'm sure they're breathing in some secret way, ". . . and you act like one, too!"

We're all dying in a good way.

When the hilarity subsides, Becky asks, "Hey, what's that song with all the verses that Tia used to sing with Zelda?"

Chad answers by launching into "Bye Bye, Miss American Pie." Good thing he chose a career in medicine.

We all join in, saying good-bye to Miss American Pie and to Tia, taking the Chevy to the levee in one group voice, a heartfelt, badly sung homage to Tia Seng.

We're wailing away, and I'm thinking maybe they can hear us at the nurses' station all the way over in the new wing, when this weird sound kicks in a one-note harmony.

High-pitched. Wailing.

A code? No, never heard an emergency code called like that.

Fire alarm?

Shane and Rick quit singing. We all do. The twins reach into their pockets. Pull out matching beepers. It's the beepers that scream the weird flat-line sound.

But it's not a flat-line sound. Quite the opposite.

"Oh, God," Becky says, and she starts shaking as she figures out what's going on.

The beepers have never sounded before. They wail for only one reason: a matching heart and lungs has come available. Their one note is saying, one of you has a chance to live. One.

Deadly silence. Chad looks ready for acute care. Becky's holding Rick for dear life. I glance at Zee. Her ghost has metastasized, there are a thousand of them dancing on her face. I go to her, take her hand. She barely notices.

The twins lock eyes. This is not a drill. I repeat, this is not a drill.

Shane reaches back into his pocket.

Out comes a coin. Big and shiny. A silver dollar.

My strange mind wonders: how long has he been carrying that thing around?

"Heads or tails, bro'?" Shane asks his brother, lazy-voiced. "Call it in the air."

Rick stares at him.

One flip of the coin. That's how you decide which brother lives and which brother dies?

Maybe, who led the more worthy life?

Who will contribute the most to the world?

Who hasn't had sex yet?

Zoey's gone full ghost. Her hand vibrates in mine.

Shane doesn't wait for Rick's call. He flips the silver dollar into the air, where it spins end over end, seems to hang forever at the top before it starts downward.

I swear it's slo-mo on its way down.

"Call it!" Shane orders his brother. "Call it!"

We all turn to Rick. What's it gonna be, heads or tails?

"Call it!" Shane repeats. "Call it!"

2
ZOEY

Schlitz.

I forget how to breathe.

Follow the bouncing silver dollar. Clang, clang, clang. It comes to rest against the wall.

Heads? Tails?

Irrelevant. Rick doesn't call it in the air.

Recall natural inhale-exhale process. My mind flies.

Faster than the speed of fright: Rick lives, Shane could die. Shane lives, Rick could die.

Faster than the speed of sight: on my way to The Secret Room, I saw Bodacious Blonde Bombshell a.k.a. Triple B roommate a.k.a. Walking Female Perfection SCRUB Summer Everly in a clothes-optional encounter full-body lock with Dr. Bradley a.k.a. Dr. B a.k.a. The Guy Who Runs This Place.

Faster Than Speeds of Light and Sight Thought #3: would Tristan care?

Faster Than Speeds of Light and Sight Thought #4: Tristan is holding my hand.

Final Faster Than Speeds of Light and Sight Thought: how deeply I suck for thinking about me-Tristan-Summer *right now*.

I look over at Shane. He ups self from wheelchair. Mosies over to fallen coin. Reaches down. Grabs it.

Spins a 180 to Rick: "It's your lucky day, butt-hole. Who says you can't call do-over?"

Rick, stone-face. Mute. Becky's right hand is a tourniquet on his upper arm.

Shane about to flip the coin again. He fixes steely eyes on his twin. "One of us is going to get a new heart and lungs in about three hours. This time you're gonna call it."

Their eyes lock. They mind wrestle. Neither moves a joint.

"Do something," I finally say. "The quicker they get one of you into surgery, the better chance the heart and lungs have of working."

From Shane: "Thank you, Zoey, for that gem of medical wisdom."

His eyes never leave Rick. "I'm flipping it. Call it in the air, Rick."

The coin flies. What goes up must . . .

Rick makes no call.

Shane's fury fills the room. "Dammit, Rick, call it!"

Nothing.

. . . come down. Clang. Clang. Clang.

Shane's hands are two white fists. "You mother!" he screams in his brother's face. "You chicken shi—"

"Take the heart and lungs, Shane," Rick says.

"What?" Becky wails.

But Rick eyes only his brother. "I want you to take it. There'll be another one soon. I just know it."

From Becky: "No!"

Now Rick turns to her. "I can't choose myself over my brother." His hand strokes her wild curls. "Could you?"

Becky's heart breaks visibly. Over love for her own brother, Jake. Who is a chronic schizophrenic back in New York City. Over her love for Rick. Over his for Shane.

Shane sneers. "For two years we've had an agreement about what we were gonna do when a heart came for one of us. And now you want to play hero in front of your new squeeze. Fine, bro'. *I'll* call it."

'Scuse me while I kiss the sky, says the sailing silver dollar. Up, up, and away.

"Tails!" Shane calls.

My hand tightens in Tristan's. At least two SCRUBS will the sucker to land "heads." Becky, for sure. And me. I admit it. For Becky. For Becky-and-Rick.

Tristan? Heads? Tails? Who knows what he wants, besides Summer?

The coin heads south. Bounces. Clang. Clang. Becky flies off the bed, bends over it.

"Thank you, God!" she cries. She flies back to the bed, laughing, crying, pulling Rick close. Rick is motionless. And Shane is smiling.

Very, very odd.

"You win, bro', fair and square," Shane declares. Apparently regret-free.

I marvel at this. Would I feel likewise for my own brother, a.k.a. Anal Retentive Lawyer, a.k.a. Anal Ree, husband of the Skank Socialite From Hell a.k.a. The Skank?

Highly doubtful.

Does Tristan love anyone that much?

"You're rockin' now, brother," Shane tells Rick, mondo expansive. "So get your butt-ugly self down to the OR so they can prep you. 'Cuz everyone knows, the better man won. Including me."

"He's right." Becky sighs, and her tears fall on Rick as she wraps herself around him. He extricates himself, kissing her forehead.

"There's something I need to do first," he says.

"Whatever it is, hurry," Becky implores him.

"It won't take long."

Rick moves slowly from bed to wheelchair. Reaches into the side bag hanging from it. I recall Snickers, 'zines, cellular phone, blah, blah.

"Rick, you really need to get down to—" Chad begins.

Rick's face clouds. "They're not here."

"What?" Becky asks.

Rick shrugs. "I've got it in my room."

Becky scrambles up. "Whatever it is, I'll wheel you back there, and then—"

"No. I want to spend a little time with Shane before the operation. Alone. He can take me. Right, Shane?"

"Right."

Becky's eyes meet mine. I signal: back off.

She turns to Shane. "You'll go back to your room quickly? And then get him down to the transplant unit?"

"Cross my heart."

That cracks all of us up. Except Rick. Maybe he's freaking. Or guilty. Or both.

Tristan suggests we exit stage right, as serious mackage ensues between Becky and Rick.

Girl parts tingle. Steam rises from the bed. Which flashes me to Triple B roommate and Dr. B again. Which flashes me to Triple B and Tristan. To me and Tristan.

Shameless Hussy. Go ahead, tattoo it on my forehead.

As we leave, Rick and Becky pull apart. Shane awaits his brother. In ten hours or so, it'll be all over.

One way or the other.

Dear Erin the Body,

Follow directions carefully: a) Remove naked bootie from Mario's manly digits. b) Remove said bootie from Italian Stallion's bearskin rug. c) Read missive. d)

Make immediate transatlantic call on Mario's dime. Lira. Whatever.

We are so not in Oklahoma anymore, girlfriend. High school grad unparty and flying bullets at Café Au Laid seem like a lifetime ago. Hot fun in the summertime. You're trolling for studs across Europe. I'm a SCRUB at Effing-Huh.

Huh? sez Erin. Effing-what?

Effing-Huh. Fable Harbor University Hospital, in quaint seaside Cape Fable, Massachusetts. I grieve for your lust-induced memory loss. Endorphins can do that.

So let's review, Okie sistuh: You called from chalet in Swiss Alps. Gave lurid details of Triple M—macho, manly, and married—Italian Stallion who picked you up in Paris and whisked you away to above. Mid-kinky phone sex detail, Triple M entered. Sounding transatlantically pissed. You hung up in my ear. I get bad feeling.

Feeling was not abated by breezy postcard with Xerox of your butt and Mario's digit. (Read: hopeful it was attached to his hand. If not, more than I needed to see. And he's a Quatro M. Add mini. At least you gave return address.)

Did you get my long letter? Morbid details of accident and Tia's death did not prompt phone call. Causing

*dangerous swelling of bad feeling in me re you. In
immortal words of Blondie: Call me.*

*Roomie Becky, madly in love with even-now-getting
heart-lung-tranplant Rick, is walking on sunshine. Stop
me before I use any more VH1-hit-wonders song titles.
Am fighting new quirk. Even as my fingers fly across
my Compaq, Rick is—*

"Zoey?"

I look up from typing my letter to Erin. Summer
stands in doorway of unsweet suite. Blond by God.
Body by Victoria's Secret. Any markings of secret
tryst with Dr. B don't show.

Shocked doesn't begin to cover it. Dr. B is
middle-aged. Married. Fatherly.

Very high ick factor there.

Summer smooths perfectly smooth hair, waits for
me to respond.

Android, I'm thinking. Looks like a woman. Talks
like a woman. But actually . . .

Flucks like a woman. Who am I kidding? Not that
I, last American virgin over age of fifteen, knows
how a woman flucks. Or soul-free Summer, for that
matter.

Read: me, insane with jealousy. The only guy I've
ever wanted wants Summer. Knows exactly how she
flucks.

"What?" My voice drips irritation.

"They're ready," says Summer, all soft southern
twang.

"I know that."

"They're wheeling Shane down to surgery in—"

"Rick," I interrupt. "You mean Rick. And I'm going over to be with Becky as soon as I—"

"I mean Shane." Summer smiles coolly. "I always say what I mean, Zoey."

I *loathe* her. "Look, I was there. You weren't. They flipped for it. Shane won."

The bitch stands there, all-knowing.

"You can't even tell them apart," I snap.

Summer, unfazed. "Try to keep up, Zoey," she says sweetly. "Shane is the one they're prepping for surgery. Rick is the one whose stomach is being pumped."

My jaw falls open.

"Rick swallowed fifteen aspirin in his bathroom to mess up his platelets so that they'd have to give Shane the transplant," she explains. "I knew you'd want to know."

I set new sprint record to Effing-Huh OR transplant unit.

There's Chad and Becky. She's sobbing. Tristan leans against wall, arms folded, head bowed.

Oh, God. Oh, no.

It's true.

I go to Tristan. "Someone"—(read: the name I speaketh not)—"just told me Rick swallowed a bunch of aspirin."

Tristan nods.

Becky pulls out of Chad's arms. "He did it so they'd have to give Shane the transplant," she cries bitterly.

"Aspirin's a blood thinner," Chad explains, which I already know. "He'd bleed too much for surgery. It gave him some tach for a while—heart jumped around like a caught fish—but he's okay. They've got him under observation and on a monitor."

"Damn him!" Becky yells.

Chad reaches for her. "He's one selfless guy, Becky. You should be proud of him."

"Well, I'm not. He's dying to save Shane," Becky sobs. "And he's killing me, too. And I hate him for it." She collapses into Chad's arms again.

I sit. Tristan joins me. Ten minutes pass silently. Summer shows. And a small, skinny African-American kid with one leg emerges from the elevator, a speed demon on his crutches. All baggy clothes and bad-ass shades. He limps with attitude.

Jerome Franklin. Age ten. Bone cancer. Top of the class at his private school. Parents with Ph.D.s But Jerome plays it like he's street. Runs the peds ward and everyone in it.

"What're you doing up here so late, Jerome?" Summer asks. She checks Rolex. Frowns. "It's past ten o'clock."

"What you think, woman?" Jerome limps over to Tristan. "The word on peds is, Shane be gettin' new spark plugs."

Tristan nods.

Jerome shakes his head. "Shoulda been my man Rick."

Tristan nods again.

"Word." Then Jerome curses. Plops into chair. Curses again.

My sentiments exactly.

Summer sits on the other side of Tristan. Her hand flutters down to his thigh.

Life is so flucking unfair.

3

TRISTAN

I'm out on my mental surfboard riding the waves when Bradley calls the meeting to order. Next to him sits Dr. Vivian Pace, the coldly beautiful, very deadly Virus.

Bradley is a throat-clearer. Ahem. Unlike The Virus, he never screams. Or belittles. He's kind, mild-mannered, and, according to Ira, brilliant. Ira doesn't throw *brilliant* around easily, either. In fact, if he hadn't told Bradley that he thinks I'm just as brilliant, I wouldn't be here.

I'll get him for that one day.

Instantly all eyes of us lowly SCRUBS are on Bradley. Because we like him, yes, but more so because—let's face it—he's The Man.

With a benign smile, Dr. B says, "I hope you all enjoyed your breakfast."

We all nod. What's not to enjoy? We got word to assemble in this windowless conference room for a catered breakfast instead of dining in our usual bastion of horror, the FHUH cafeteria. We've sucked up an excellent spread: fresh baked goods, a variety of cheeses and jams, three kinds of juice, even coffee on the verge of drinkability.

Something must be up. Because we SCRUBS, even minus our usual hideous reds, definitely do not rate this.

Am I curious? In some minor way.

Really, I'm thinking if I can't be out hanging ten, it's a glorious Thursday to be marooned indoors. Because Shane made it through surgery just fine. Hours one to twenty-four post-transplant are intensely tricky. Your rib cage has just been hacked open by surgeons, your T-cells are aching to engage in extreme fighting with your newly arrived organs, and all you've got between you and the land of Tia Seng is intravenous cyclosporin.

Organ rejection is an exceptionally painful way to die.

But Shane is rejecting rejection, we hear. Rick hangs in, too, already over his overdose. He's even visited Shane. Would've loved to be a potted plant at *that* reunion.

I one-two the conference oval. To my left is Summer, a vision in gray cashmere. Her eyes beam brightly at Dr. B. Who could escape that radiance?

She's minus last night's De Rien, her signature scent, but she never wears it to work.

I smell it anyway. On my own skin. In my own mind.

Next to her is Bradley. Then The Virus. How can a woman that beautiful be less appealing than the three-hundred-pound beauty queen of the ER, Selma the cleaning woman, whose front teeth boast her gold-plated initials?

And yet, she is.

Next to Pace is an empty chair.

Then Chad, Becky, Zee. The ghost has retreated from Zoey, I notice. Although there's always something a little haunted in her eyes. And, at the moment, crumbs on her face. She has put away massive amounts of food, per usual.

The girl can chew.

Becky puts her finger to her own mouth, makes sweeping motions, and eyes Zoey, who gets the hint and quickly brushes herself clean.

I liked the crumbs better.

"Dr. Pace and I asked you to join us here for breakfast this morning," Bradley begins, "because we've got a guest whom we wanted you all to meet." He glances at his watch. "He said he'd be here at 9:04. And if I know Dr. Coolidge, that means—"

The wall clock ticks once, to 9:04, as the conference room door opens.

Tall, African-American, and handsome walks in.

"Ah, Dr. Coolidge." Dr. Bradley rises, as does The Virus. "Thank you for taking time out of your busy schedule to come meet these young people. SCRUBS, I'd like you to meet Dr. Martin Coolidge. He recently joined us at FHUH to head up our organ transplantation team, and we consider ourselves most fortunate to have him. Dr. Coolidge, meet the SCRUBS."

I see Becky's eyes go wide, and she leans over to Chad. She whispers, "He operated on—"

"Ms. Silver," Dr. Pace says, in her best first-grade teacher voice. "Please."

Becky reddens as Dr. Coolidge takes the empty seat next to The Virus. His walk is purposeful, his bearing ramrod military. Ex–Army Ranger? Navy SEAL? Marines?

Objectively, he's world-class handsome. Six-one or two, one-eighty or so, BMI under 8. Either the guy lives in the gym or chews Orlistat like Chicklets. A more chiseled version of Will Smith—even I, hater of mass media, can reference Will—with a little Denzel thrown in for good measure.

Chad gets nervous. I know how he thinks: *another guy Eve would choose over me.* He's forever comparing himself to other guys, and forever finding himself wanting. But then in Chad's mind, Chad is still his own "before" picture.

I'm checking out The Virus checking out Dr. Coolidge. Those stone-cold eyes glint like she's picturing Coolidge and her and a billiards table. And she'll break the balls, thanks.

But I don't think she can break his. He's Dr. Cool.

"Dr. Coolidge performed the heart-lung transplant surgery yesterday on Shane Carr," Bradley confirms. "He's the youngest transplant surgeon in the western world, actually. Thirty-two. Isn't that correct, Dr. Coolidge?"

"Yes, sir. That's correct, sir."

Military "yes, sir." Bingo.

"Each of you will have an opportunity, in the near future, to work closely with Dr. Coolidge and to observe him in the operating theater." Dr. B scans the table to see that we're suitably impressed by this. We are.

"Dr. Coolidge's background is a fascinating one," Dr. B continues. "I wonder if you might be persuaded to share some of it with these young people, Dr. Coolidge."

Dr. Cool turns to Bradley. "Sir, with all due respect, sir, exactly who are these *children*? And what are they doing in our hospital?"

Dr. B turns to The Virus, frowning. "Dr. Pace?"

"I thought *you* were going to be briefing Dr. Coolidge," she says.

It's the first time I've seen Bradley pissed. Also the first time I've seen The Virus flustered.

But she rallies and smoothly explains the SCRUBS program, about how we five were selected from ten thousand applicants from across North America because of our aptitude for and interest in medicine, et cetera, et cetera.

When told a story, most Americans give nonverbal reactions as a sign of interest. Inupiat Eskimos do not.

Neither does Dr. Cool.

This further flusters The Virus. She then launches into an unintentionally hilarious speech about how excited she is to be working with us, how we're a team, how exciting it is that at the end of the summer, one of us will be awarded a twenty-five-thousand-dollar scholarship.

Right.

She loathes us but only allows it to show when Dr. B isn't around.

It's everything I can do not to fall over laughing.

Dr. Cool sits motionless. Finally he turns to Dr. B. "Sir, who receives this scholarship?"

"Whomever the benefactor chooses," Dr. B. responds.

"And, sir, the benefactor is—?" Cool asks.

"The benefactor wishes to remain anonymous," says The Virus.

Anonymous. That's all we know. But Summer's mouth turns up at the corners. Interesting.

The Virus pushes a folder toward him, which says SCRUBS on the cover. He scans it while we wait. He looks up once, his eyes meet mine. Then he turns to Dr. B. "I'll review some of my background for the SCRUBS now, sir," he says.

Dr. B nods.

Then Dr. Cool's eyes home in on mine like a cruise missile. What the hell is in that folder he just sped-read?

"I was raised in Oakland, California," Dr. Cool begins, all crisp consonants and flat affect. "I had two brothers. One is in San Quentin doing time for felony murder, and no, he was not jailed unjustly. The other was killed ten years ago. Six bullets from a Glock in a drive-by. And yes, he was killed unjustly. I entered college at sixteen, did two years, then served in special ops in the Marines, following which I completed my undergraduate studies and my medical training at Harvard."

His eyes have not moved. Neither have mine. Fine. We'll engage in some mutual iridology. Dr. Cool is used to winning. Easily. Not this time. Sir.

"Med school, surgery residency, and here," he concludes tersely. "That's it. Any questions?"

Even Chad is smart enough this time to keep his hand down.

"No questions?" Dr. Cool asks. "That's unfortunate. A marvelous opportunity missed." He looks at his watch. "I'm due in the OR in forty-five." He stands up and just short of a salute says, "Thank you for inviting me in, Dr. Bradley."

"Thank you, Dr. Coolidge," Dr. Bradley says. "I'll walk you out."

The two of them leave, and no sooner does the door click shut than The Virus jumps up and goes ballistic.

"Do you realize what an opportunity you idiots just missed?" she screams. "Dr. Martin Coolidge is going to win a Nobel prize someday. He was profiled in *Time* last year. Dr. Coolidge asked you: Any questions? That means you—?"

"Ask questions?" Chad ventures into the thick silence.

The Virus rolls her eyes and looks at the ceiling like she's got a direct line to the Great Big Doctor in the Sky and is now commiserating with Him about our stupidity.

"Get out of here. All of you," she commands.

Her order is our command. We're almost out when she adds, "Except Silver."

Becky stops, we keep going. Slowly.

"No, I changed my mind," The Virus decides. "You go, too, Silver. But if I ever hear that you are engaging in a relationship with a patient that is unbecoming to the profession to which you aspire but will most likely never achieve, buy yourself a bus ticket back to New York City. No. Hitchhike. Is that clear?"

"Yes, but I . . ." Becky has nowhere to go but down.

"But you what?" The Virus looms over her in mile-high stiletto heels.

"I heard you, Dr. Pace," Becky manages.

I'm pretty sure we won't find Becky in The Secret Room with Rick Carr anytime soon.

Hours later I'm a hundred yards off the beach, catching little three-foot rollers and riding them for all they're worth. Which isn't much. Got my new wet suit on. The ocean here is cold. Not the bathtub temps of Hawaii I'm used to. But in the wet suit, I'm toasty.

I can just hear Stevie telling me what a wuss I am. He'd go in buck-naked at dawn in December just to rag on me.

The late afternoon sun feels great, and the beach is nearly deserted. I turn and paddle out some more, see my wave coming, spin the board, and I'm up on my feet, right in the crest. Cut some turns, left, right, left, up over the crest and back down. Yeah! Good one. For Massachusetts.

Kick out, ready to paddle back when I see another surfer at the waterline. Long board. Wet suit.

Very female.

Zoey?

I hop the next wave and ride it all the way in.

"Hey," she says. Very casual. Well, what did I expect, blatant joy at seeing me? I check her eyes. Momentarily ghost-free.

"Hey. Where'd you get the board and the wet suit?"

She waves vaguely toward town. "Rental shop."

I nod. Once I offered to teach her to surf. Once she accepted. But then she told me she found another teacher. Evidently the idea of spending that much time with me didn't appeal. But then how do you explain the incredible time we had when we went kamikaze snowboarding together? Yes, in June. On Mount Washington. She loved it, for real. I'm sure of it.

I squint into the dying sun. "You know what you're doing?"

"Is that question asked in the existential sense, or does it refer to surfing?"

"Same difference."

She gives new meaning to an arched eyebrow, then looks around. "Amazing. My instructor didn't show just because I told him that I couldn't afford to pay him."

"So, you were hoping I'd spontaneously offer?"

The Zee's eyes narrow. She's ticked, even though I meant to be funny. "Forget it—"

"I'd like to teach you, Zoey. Really. How many lessons have you had so far?"

She holds up the OK sign with her thumb and forefinger. Meaning, in this case, zero.

I ponder. She's an athlete, ace snowboarder, serious swimmer. And she's got a longboard, easy to learn on. Should pick it right up. I've learned all the above through experience. Surfing's not at all hard. And if you happen to fall, water's not hard, either. Unless your neck contacts bottom or a reef and you snap it.

Well, as Stevie would say, them's the breaks.

The guy has a real sick sense of humor.

I nod. "Put your board down and let's get started."

She drops her board to the sand. I put mine alongside it and launch into a crash course about safety, riptides, paddling, bending knees, turning, and staying back on your board. I make no cute moves to use teaching her as an excuse to hold that lovely narrow waist. In fact, I don't touch her at all. I've seen her in much less than a wet suit. But still.

There's something about Zee in full-body black latex rubber.

She's staring at me, arms folded, in total jock girl mode. Fine. Moving on.

"So, that's about it. It's like snowboarding, really," I conclude. "Let me see your form."

She climbs onto her board, prone. Gets to halfway position, then pops full up. Stands normal, not goofy-footed. Knees bent, balanced, centered. All right.

Fable Harbor surfing is not exactly the Banzai Pipeline on the North Shore of Hawaii, where more than once I've found myself in the middle of a tube, looking at a big fish suspended in the crest of a wave as it breaks over me. The rush is so intense, it always makes me want more, higher, harder, bigger, riskier.

Now, that's surfing.

But back to here. And now. Zoey's got one hand on her hip and an impatient "well?" in her eyes.

"Let's see it again. Your form."

This merits a sigh. "My *form*, Tristan, is on the tall side, on the thin side, and you've seen it enough on the dry side. Can we just get into the water? This is not brain surgery."

I agree. On one condition.

"You got Sex Wax?" I ask her innocently.

She reddens. Knew she would.

"Do I have *what*?"

"Sex Wax. Can't go surfing without Sex Wax. It's a rule."

"That is so not funny."

"Maybe because I was so not trying to be," I say. I pull said Sex Wax out of my small pack and hand it to her.

"What's it say on the can?" I ask.

"It says Tristan March is in love with . . ." She holds the can closer, pretending like it's hard to read. ". . . Tristan March."

I contemplate her. "Is that what you think? Really?"

"We playing guessing games or are we surfing?" she snaps.

Fine. I know a leave-me-alone when I hear it.

I drop to my knees and massage Sex Wax into the top of her longboard. "This makes your feet stick to your board," I explain, all business.

We tether our ankles to our boards and wade in. Zee feels the cold, I can tell, but she won't show it, and soon her body heats up under her wet suit as the two of us paddle out, side by side. She paddles like a pro, like she's been doing it all her life.

Has the girl been shining me on? Nah. She's from Oklahoma. Lousy waves there.

We get out to where the waves are primo, relatively speaking, turn our boards, and sit up.

"Listen up," I tell her. "You pick your wave, paddle like we did on the beach, let it catch you, and stand up. Don't be intimidated by—"

Before I finish the sentence, Zee is gone.

She's paddling madly. The wave's catching her. It's got her. Or else she has it, 'cuz it's the moment of truth. She's on one knee. Wobbling a little, and . . . All right! She's up! And she's ridin' it!

It's like I can feel it with her, like I'm inside of her. The first time is just so—

"Go, Zee!" I cheer.

Amazing. I'm seriously impressed. A first-wave rider. I wasn't one. Even Billie wasn't one. And she's the best female on a board I've ever seen.

I catch the next one and follow Zee in. She kicks out sideways like we practiced on the beach, and I kick out, too, and the two of us are whooping and splashing like a coupla kids.

"This is fantastic!" she cries, breathing hard. Her eyes are on fire. Her body. This is just how she must look when she's—

"More," she declares. And she's paddling back out again.

For the next hour, until the light starts to fade, we surf. She loses that edge, gets all playful, like we're both ten years old, with nothing more on our minds than making the summer last forever.

Zee gets cocky, moves a little forward on her board—big mistake but inevitable, really, it happens to everyone—she sinks the tip, and is rewarded with a headfirst launch into the ocean.

Gone. My heart turns over. Zee? Zee?

But then she's there, waving her arms to show she's fine, and draws a finger across her throat to say she's ready to pack it in.

Two minutes later we're sitting on the beach, catching our breath, reliving her triumph. She is incandescent with joy. Perfect. I wonder if she has any idea.

"I could get hooked on that," she says, swiping her wet hair off her face.

"I already am."

"Is the surfing better in Hawaii?"

I laugh. "In comparison, this is an icy bathtub."

"Then I want to surf there." She glows at the thought, throws her head back to the last of the sun. "Maybe I should have picked a future profession that involves sun and surf," she murmurs.

"You don't have to become a doctor."

"Yeah, I do."

I'm on one elbow, regarding the beautiful line of her neck. "Did I miss that one in *Zoey's Rulebook of Life?*"

"It's not a rule." She opens her eyes and looks at me. "More like a promise. One I made a long time ago."

"To who?"

She sifts some sand through her fingers, doesn't answer.

"You get to change the rules if you want, Zoey," I point out.

She sits up. "I don't want. And now it's time for a *Tristan's Rulebook of Life* question."

"Next time," I say much more easily than how I feel. Time to change the subject. "You want to—"

"This time." She regards me thoughtfully. "You told me your mom lives in Hawaii, which is where you learned to surf, and your dad lives in Alaska, which is where you learned to ski. And you love both."

"Excellent recall." I'm going from ill at ease to dis-ease. How ironically appropriate. "So, Zoey, let's get out of these—"

"You're not getting out of anything," she says. And I'm nailed. "You love sports. Risky sports. I got that. They make you feel alive. Got that, too. So what I'm wondering is . . . have you ever loved a person like that?"

4

ZOEY

Holy schlitz. Did I really just ask him that?

Message to self: staple mouth shut.

I study Tristan's face. Feign attitude of semi-comatose detachment. Realize he's debating answering me.

How coy.

Then he barely nods. Then—

"Yo, Zoey! Tristan!"

Coy-tus interruptus. In the person of Leo Seng. Who bounds across the beach in our direction.

Skinny, funny Leo. Cambodian ancestry, American 'tude. Townie. Hospital orderly, temporarily. His plan: save bucks to make break for Hollywood and motion picture stardom as last action hero.

Dr. Victoria Seng, a.k.a. The Anti-Virus, a.k.a. Fave Rave Doc of Effing-Huh, is his big sister.

His other big sister was Tia Seng.

Leo waves at us. Baggy jammers fall below his nonwaist, his eyes hidden behind wraparound shades. Lagging behind him are two bikini-clad girls and a bald guy with muscles on his muscles.

Tristan's on his feet. Thus endeth Q & A. I rise, too.

" 'Zup?" Leo bumps Tristan's fist. "Nice out there today, huh?" Leo cocks his head toward the sea.

"Decent," says Tristan.

I admit I have no basis of comparison.

"Too cool, I love virgins!" Leo laughs too loud. Launches into mindless manic monologue about mind-numbing minutiae of life.

A memory: Teenie-Zoey—first grade?—in the hallway of my parents' medical office. Per usual I need to tell them something *now*. But they're with Rose Ember's mother. Per usual, I eavesdrop. Rose's mother going on about stupid things like her garden and her famous meat-loaf recipe and all the nice cards she got after Rose's funeral. Rose, age eight. Darted around a parked car to see if the school bus was coming. It was. She died under massive wheels.

Same night, dinnertime. It wasn't right for Rose's mom to be talking about her famous meat-loaf recipe right after Rose's death, I decree to my parents. And besides, *their own daughter* had needed them. But they were too busy listening to Rose's mom's *famous meat-loaf recipe.*

"Everyone grieves differently," my mother explained. "Mrs. Ember grieves by talking."

My father sips wine, adds, "When someone you love dies, any reaction you might have to it short of suicide is acceptable, Zoey. You see?"

Didn't like it. But I saw.

So. Leo grieves by talking, too.

But. My parents really listened to Mrs. Ember. I only *pretend* to listen to Leo. But. Someday I will be the kind of doctor both my parents were.

And grief is just . . . I don't grieve.

I act.

Mid-story about Party Central, the dilapidated beach house Leo rents, Twin Bikinis and Shaved Headed World Gym wander over. Intros happen. Tisha Henry and Allie Drew suck cancer sticks with the desperation of new high school grads never farther from Fable Harbor than Boston. Shaggy brunettes who look enough alike to be sisters.

Both reek of trying too hard. Both baby fat skinny.

Read: zip food, zip exercise, lots o' nicotine.

Shaved Head World Gym is Greg Reese. Effing-Huh Emergency Medical Technician and Zen Buddhist. Earrings in both ears and muscles stained by pink sunset. He grins. It fits his face. Unlike the NicoTwins, he's comfortable in his own skin. Zen Greg.

Zen Greg shines that smile on me.

Meaningfully.

Well. My eyes slide to Tristan. Hope rises that he a) notices; b) gets it; and c) is insanely jealous.

Actual result? D) none of the above.

Hope loses stiffie.

Leo relaunches mindless manic monologue, decides to get Frisbee from car, sprints off into the dying of the light. NicoTwin #1 in daisy-print bikini sidles closer to Tristan. Sucks up carcinogens. Exhales perfect smoke ring and smiles at Tristan.

Meaningfully.

"Wanna butt?" she offers.

"Don't smoke," Tristan replies.

"I quit for like, six months," the other NicoTwin pipes up. "I just started again."

Uh-huh.

"But I'm gonna quit again," she goes on. "I only smoke, like, three cigs a day now."

Can actually feel my brain cells begin to atrophy.

"Me, I do, like, two, three packs a day," NicoTwin Daisy Print adds. "I'm like totally addicted."

More brain cells expire.

"So, you like to surf?" NicoTwin Daisy, the addicted smoker, asks Tristan.

"More than I like to breathe," says Tristan.

"Wow, me, too!" NicoTwin Daisy's voice is awe-filled. As if discovering a common interest in, say, Jackson Pollock's earliest work. She inhales Tristan on her next drag.

"It's such a rush. Like great sex, you know?"

He knows. And I know that look on his face. Beyond flirting. Tristan doesn't flirt. More like . . . intense focus. I've seen him do it with women over and over again. All ages, all types, ashes, ashes, all fall down.

An equal opportunity ego-rush.

He focuses on NicoTwin Daisy. It's infinitely hotter than flirting.

Yep. NicoTwin Daisy is melting.

"I heard you guys will be on the flying bus with us sometime soon," Zen Greg says to me.

I tear my eyes away from NicoTwin Daisy's mating dance.

"Flying bus?"

"Ambulance," Greg fills in. "We EMTs got notes about it from The Virus."

I laugh. "Does everyone call her that?"

"Only those who know her. So, where are you from, Zoey?"

Love that small talk. It's so . . . small.

"Oklahoma."

"Anywhere near Oklahoma City?"

" 'Burbs of." I'm only half-listening. NicoTwin Daisy is laughing, leaning floral-covered right nipple against Tristan's same-side forearm.

Subtle.

"OKC's been through a lotta nasty stuff, huh?" Greg says. "Killer tornadoes. Bombing of the Murrah Building—that was unreal. I was there."

My head snaps toward him. "You were—?"

He nods. "There's a Zen retreat out in the middle of nowhere, near Sallislaw, believe it or not. Heard about the bombing on the radio I wasn't supposed to be listening to while chowing down the burger I wasn't supposed to be eating. So I got on my Harley and gunned it, was there in under two hours. Figured an EMT could help."

I could say, "Funny, my parents were there, too. Dad died instantly. You couldn't have helped him. But my mother. Trapped under there. Calling. Bleeding to death. You could have helped her."

Nah.

"Hey, you okay?" Greg asks, lightly touching my arm.

"Fine."

"You looked upset just now, is why I asked," Greg explains. "Makes sense. It's your hometown."

"No, it isn't."

His eyes question me.

I could say, "My real home is Cheney, OK, population 8,423." Or tell what happened after my parents were buried. How Anal Ree and The Skank sold the home that my great-grandfather had built. Made me move to their home in the vomitous burbs, unhappily ever after, where the horror flick of Mom under rubble calling me to help her and I can't move can't breathe can't anything plays nightly in the theater of my mind. Still.

Nah.

Greg nods. Knows enough to back off. Is okay with it.

"Oh, so you know about the bomb?" NicoTwin Daisy is asking Tristan, all breathy and eager.

Huh? She's talking about Oklahoma City, too?

NicoTwin Dots laughs, waves homegrown pink-manicured nails. "He doesn't know what you're talking about, Tish."

Neither do I. Although now I do know that NicoTwin Daisy is Tisha. Tisha explains that *bomb* is local slang for *bon*. No, not French *bon*. Not that good. Fable *Havre* bon. As in "bonfire." As in mega-beach party.

"Saturday night," she concludes, shaking hair off her face. Eyes half-closed, to Tristan: "You should come."

And he will, I think. On Summer's arm. Not yours. You are so no comp for Female Perfection.

Leo has sprinted back, spins his glow-in-the-dark Frisbee on the tip of one finger. "Yeah, man," he agrees. "Should be wild." He snaps the Frisbee to Greg.

"Noble partying," Greg says on a between-the-legs catch. "It's a fund-raiser for breast cancer research."

A light dawns. It's a charity thing. Didn't Tia once mention doing volunteer work for them?

But Leo leaves that unspoken, so I do, too.

Tristan's eyes meet mine. He's thinking the same thing, I know it.

Funny how I can read his thoughts.

Funny how he never answered my question.

Much later, in our unsweet in the med school dorm. Becky is elsewhere. With Rick in The Secret Room and fluck The Virus. Dangerous. Summer's in the bathroom doing endless whatever. I lie on my bed reading a book from the med library about Tourette's syndrome. Hope to score points with whichever big cheese takes us on peds rounds the next morning.

That thus far The Virus has ranked Tristan and The Perfect One above me rankles.

I will beat them. I will be number one. I will win the twenty-five-thousand dollars. Because I will simply work harder than they do.

That's how I got here. That's how I'll get there. I read:

Tourette's syndrome is a physical disorder of the brain which usually manifests in childhood. Causation unknown, however several studies link syndrome with an excess of, or hypersensitivity to, the brain chemical dopamine. Manifestation of Tourette's includes symptomatic involuntary movements, i.e., motor tics and involuntary vocalizations such as, but not limited to, eye blinking, head jerking, repetitive hand movements, sniffing, grunting, mirroring other's speech, or cursing.

Involuntary cursing? Filter-free Schlitz?

Could I have a mild case?

I read on, fascinated by the bizarreness of it. There's method to my madness: a kid with Tourette's and weird-o fever was admitted today. Jerome's new roommate. Fever usually from infection, infection usually curable, which is why he was admitted.

The Tourette's? Un-uh.

Having one or the other isn't enough? Love those cosmic jokes with no punch line.

Becky floats in on sea of love, all smiles and sighs.

"Listen to this," I say, my head still buried in the book. " 'Case study number three. Bruce P., age eighteen. When he and his girlfriend have inter-course, Bruce reports inability to stop himself from barking in her ear, after which he sings the theme song from *The Brady Bunch* and blinks repeatedly while yelling "Marsha, Marsha, Marsha!" ' "

"That's nice," says Becky, falling onto her bed.

No. Not nice. Strange. Sicko funny. Becky has a notoriously bent sense of humor, yet Bruce P. elicits nary a secret chuckle.

"I see you have sex-induced IDD," says I.

"IDD?"

"IQ Deficit Disorder."

"Mmmmm." She's staring at the ceiling like it's cute.

"You were . . . this is just a wild guess . . . in The Secret Room with Rick?"

Her head swivels in my direction. "He's going to get his transplant. Soon. I just know it. I love him too much for him not to get it. The power of love is limitless, you know?"

I cringe at rhetorical query of a bad self-help book. But then, what do I know about love? Less than less.

"Why'd you leave him?"

"This floater, Ann Marie, was doing night shift on peds," Becky explains. "Hirsute slipped us word that Ann Marie is The Virus's spy. So Rick went back to his room, and here I am."

Good. Out of The Virus's clutches. I study blissed-out Becky, all golden skin, voluptuous curves, wild curls.

Half Caucasian Jewish and half African-American Baptist, Becky looks Latina. I told her once that no one in my white-on-white OKC burb looked like her. She said everyone in her caramel Spanish Harlem neighborhood did.

Becky is the greatest thing since Erin left to troll for Eurostuds.

I hold up the book so she can read the title, *Tourette's Syndrome and Its Manifestations*. A future shrink, Becky is deeply into the strange. And Tourette's is right up there with Alien Hand Syndrome, where your own hand ignores your brain's signals. Hits you in chin with right uppercuts. Tries to strangle you.

Seriously. It exists. Becky told me about it.

"Tourette's should be right up your alley," I note. She sighs.

Bad sign. My minor concern veers toward major. The Virus would be only too glad to issue Becky's "yer out!"

Female Perfection begins to hum "Summertime" in the bathroom. I sit up as gag reflex kicks in. Squelch gag.

"Listen, Becky, I am not a 'get into your business' kind of friend," is how I begin, "but—"

But nothing.

Because Summer the hummer sashays out of the bathroom, looking spit-polished. Triple B glow. All blond hair, Darryl B. white jeans, Ralph Lauren white shirt. Plus pearls. Probably handed down from some fabulously rich descendant who wore them when Jefferson Davis proclaimed how the South would rah-yuz again.

I assess facts.

One, it's close to midnight.

Two, Summer has no visible panty line.

Conclusion: under designer casual wear is silk G-string and matching bra.

Summer is definitely not dressed for bed.

Correction. Not *this* bed.

"Well, I'm off," she sings as Rolex slips onto slender wrist.

"Late date?" Out of my mouth, unbidden. Can't take it back.

Summer taps one finger against her lips, studies me.

"You aren't altogether hopeless, Zoey."

"What's that supposed to mean?" Becky asks, lifted from stupor on my behalf.

Summer shrugs. "Grooming counts, Zoey. Especially for those unfortunates who are less than genetically gifted."

She smiles. "I'll give him your regards. Night, ladies." And she's out the door.

Him. Tristan?

Him. Dr. B?

"Beyond loathing," I say.

"Beyond." Becky yawns. She pads toward bathroom, trailing clothes as she goes.

When she comes out, I'll tell her about Summer and Dr. B. A neat segue, really, into her own high-risk behavior and why she has to chill with Rick.

Could work.

A soft knock.

"Beck?" someone calls through the door.

Chad. I let him in. He's so cute, nice, smart, real. Why can't I be crazed for him instead of his roommate?

"Sorry," says ever-considerate Chad. "Is it too late for company?"

I shake my head. "Becky's in the—"

"Hey," Becky greets him, post-flush. She's stripped down to camisole and panties, but she and Chad are like brother and sister. He looks only at her eyes.

But he does pace. *Très dépaysé.*

"What would you think if you got a note that said, 'You are the loveliest creature who ever walked the face of the Earth, because your beauty shines from within. Signed, Your Secret Admirer.'?"

"That someone likes me?" Becky ventures.

Funny.

"You have a secret admirer?" I ask Chad.

Sheepishly he confides, "I sort of am one."

"And you never told me?" Becky objects, punching Chad in the arm before launching herself toward her bed.

Perfect three-point landing.

"It's complicated."

"Details," Becky demands.

Chad puffs out air, sits next to her. "Back in Chicago, when I was this five-foot-nothing geek, there was this amazing woman training to be a physical therapist who worked with our B-ball team. I was too short to play, so I managed the team. She's the one who got me interested in sports medicine. We got to be great friends."

"And?" Becky asks.

"And . . . she left. And then I grew, thank God."

"And got very cute," Becky adds.

"Unfortunately, she never saw that part." He assumes classic far-off look of boyish longing.

"*And?*" I prompt.

"And she's a physical therapist now."

Becky and I continue staring. As in *and?*

"Here," Chad adds.

Huh?

"Meaning Effing-Huh?" I ask.

Chad nods. "Exactly. The truth is, I was madly in love with her back then. And I still am. And she has no idea."

Becky whoops with delight. "You studboy! You followed her here, didn't you? I am so proud—"

"Not exactly—"

"You applied for SCRUBS because she's working here?" I guess.

"I love medicine, don't get me wrong," Chad protests.

"Busted!" Becky shrieks, tickling him. "What's her name? When do we meet her? I have to check out if she's good enough for you."

"I think you missed a salient detail," points out *moi,* ever the party pooper. "She doesn't know Chad's here."

"She doesn't even know I got beyond five feet two," Chad adds, going morose. "So I thought an anonymous note might—"

"Might prove that you're non-kosher chicken-schlitz," Becky says. "Just call her up, tell her you're here, meet her, and throw your manly arms around her!"

Chad betrays his Irish roots. He turns green.

"When I think about her, I feel like I'm still that dweeby kid. Like that's who she'll still see. And that would break my heart."

Okay, the guy is sweet. Truly. That guileless Chad and enigmatic Tristan are roommates and friends amuses to no end.

"I think the note is a good idea," I decide.

"Yeah?" Chad goes puppy-dog hopeful.

"Yeah. Definitely."

We both look over at Becky. Who finally relents.

"It lacks a certain grand passion, but okay," she opines. "And after this note, you leave another one saying that her secret admirer wants to meet her.

And then, you hear the bootie call of love. I weep. And I want photos."

He bops her with a pillow. She counter-bops. They're giggling and pillow fighting as I head for the bathroom.

It still smells of Summer's impossibly expensive French perfume, De Rien. Which loosely translates to, No Biggie.

But then, the bitch is different.

I do the do, lean over sink to wash my hands, and promptly elbow Becky's makeup mirror so it falls. Down. Down. I try the kick-save-it's-a-beauty to forestall seven years of smashed mirror bad luck, and the mirror falls into the trash can.

No shatter. Thank God.

I reach to retrieve it, shoving aside used tissues and other moist fallout, and my hand touches glass. A cylinder.

Up it comes, after Becky's mirror.

Whoa.

It's an empty bottle of smell-alike perfume called No Reason.

"If you like the smell of De Rien but not the price . . ."

With Female Perfection, I have no shame.

I open the meds cabinet. There sits Summer's full bottle of De Rien, clear with a gold top.

Yesterday, that bottle was half-full.

5
TRISTAN

e-mail
From: stevedaman@aol.com
To: tristmarch@juno.com
Re: Cosmic jokes

Yo yo yo and a bottle of rum. Exactly what I feel like drowning my sorrows in. Would have said bottle oh rum but I learned threw bitter experience that the voice recognizer system on my puter hates contractions and abbreviations and apostrophes of all kinds. In sum ways I like the puter voice better than mine. Talking wears me out also I have this weird tremor in my voice from the tumor and sound like I am vibrating all the time. Life is sum kind of cosmic joke. God must be into black comedy in a major way. I am shore you want news from north shore Hawaii. I am feeling the after effects now of the radiation. Well more like you can see the after effects because now my head looks as pink round and bald as Billie's butt. She would kill me if she read that and take no prisoners. Member when we said she would mellow out when she got older? We were wrong. On the surfing side Billie won the north sure invitational again and five thousand bucks and she beat guys to do it again. She has been hanging with Lark Simms of all creatures. Lark has eyes on Billie and I am not saying where. You know Lark she collects male and female scalps from every part of the anatomy. I warned Billie but she sad she can handle it but she is full of sheet. They are talking about going to Australia to surf. Scary. If you were here you could get Billie back on track. She misses you bad. She sad she sent you a postcard did you get it? I am down for the count bro so I will write more later. When you are doing the wild thing with Summer think of me every twenty seconds or so. Even if a woman were into me right now witch no woman is, twenty seconds is probably about how long I wood last.

Learn a lot and do something good with it, man.

Just realized this cosmic joke has no punch line.

Stevedaman

e-mail
From: tristmarch@juno.com
To: stevedaman@aol.com
Re: walk on the weird side

Stevie—

Whoa. Your e-mail was a weird lightning bolt from home. My guess is your new bald look just makes you look dangerous. Women love that, so don't despair. As for the twenty seconds thing, you always underestimate yourself. But if you have any change in how you're feeling, do not e-mail me, call me, faster than immediately, okay? As for Billie, she's a big girl now. After all she and I have been through, she has to make decisions for herself now, even if they suck. No, I didn't get her postcard. I'll call her. Somehow. Sometime. Maybe.

Here's my humorous FHUH story o' the day. I was up at dawn to surf before injecting myself into the usual circus at Effing-Huh. It's a ritual with me. The beach is empty, I have the waves (more like wavelets) to myself. I ease out of the suite so as not to wake Chad, my roommate, board in arms and wetsuit already on. So today I get to deserted beach, put down board to wax up, feel someone watching me. Summer keeps saying she's going to catch me out there one morning and drag me to the dunes for some early-morning delight. Or Zoey, maybe. She took to surfing like Billie took to Jose Cuervo. I turn around. It's Chad, dressed in Chicago Bulls sweats, footwear-free, carrying a notebook and a pen. So I figure maybe he's a closet poet who gets inspired by the awesome sunrise; you never know anything about anyone by looking. Remember in one e-mail I told you all about him and his massive crush on this physical therapist, Eve Carrier, from his hometown? He's finally getting up the nerve to send her an anonymous love letter. Came to the beach so I could help him rewrite it for the zillionth time. I tell him, "Chad, write like you talk." He falters. Then, "Chad, one day you're going to look in the mirror and see that the guy looking back looks good. Really good. You're not a geek kid anymore. Women at the hospital are checking you out all the time." He doesn't see it, he tells me. The truth is, even if he did see it, he doesn't care. He burns only for Eve. I think of him now as Don Quixote d'Effing-Huh. It's touching. And no, you don't get a copy of his love letter, you heathen cynic of true romance. And don't bother reminding me that romantic love eludes me. Or me, it. Keep me posted on what Dr. Ira says. And tell Billie—oh, hell. I'll call her and tell her myself . . . sometime when I get up the nerve to hear her voice.

Love,
Trist

We SCRUBS are walking stop signs. I think again, what mental midget picked red for our unis? We gather around Dr. Vic in front of the main peds nursing station, to embark on Friday morning rounds. Two new third-year med students in white coats shoot looks at us like we smell of unwashed GOMER.

I smile. After a while you get kind of cheerful about everyone hating your guts.

Dr. Vic looks over a chart. As always, she's perfectly groomed, hair tied in a glossy knot. But the stress lines around her eyes are new. There's bottomless sadness in her eyes. Her little sister, Tia, is dead. A horrible accident. No time to say good-bye. Yet she's just supposed to go on.

There's no manual on how to do that. I didn't find one, anyway.

At least Dr. Vic knows Tia's death wasn't her fault. Whereas I . . .

Whereas I carry on. Ride the weenie wavelets. Don't call Billie.

Dr. Vic is all-business as we gather around her, her face a beautiful Kabuki mask.

Doesn't anyone else see that? I glance at the other SCRUBS. No.

"The presenting patient is Bishop Wilson. Bishop is age ten, Caucasian. He was admitted with an FOUO. Which is . . . Mr. Arnold?"

She eyes the med students.

"Fever of unknown origin," says Jerrad Arnold, whose hair and freckles are exactly the shade of rust.

I see Chad's disappointment that she didn't ask him, 'cuz he had that one nailed.

"Correct," Dr. Vic asserts. "Bishop's mother reported that Bishop has been running a fever for three weeks. He tires easily, has little appetite, complains of a sore throat. How do we proceed, Ms. Urser?"

Wilma Urser is short and round, with a mouth so wide kids must have ragged her about it mercilessly. She covers it a lot with her hand. She has the most beautiful blue eyes set deep in a face that aspires to plain.

And she's a red hot. Overprepared, always.

Humor is a foreign concept.

"Following a detailed uptake to ascertain exposure to possible causatives, tests that are basically a process of elimination," Wilma reels off.

"Exactly," Dr. Vic agrees. "We'll be testing Bishop for mononucleosis, hepatitis—"

"Excuse me, Dr. Vic," Wilma interrupts. "Those tests were done yesterday."

Dr. Vic smiles tightly. "No. You misunderstood, Ms. Urser. We will also—"

"I have it here in my notes," Wilma insists, her voice rising half an octave. "Those tests were already done on this patient."

She holds a notebook out to Dr. Vic.

Dr. Vic opens her chart again, scans it. "Yes, I misspoke, Ms. Urser. Thank you for bringing that to my attention."

Misspoke? Dr. Vic never misspeaks.

Crack one in the mask, call the umpire.

"Today you were going to explain the patient's syndrome that exacerbates and complicates diagnosis and procedure," Wilma adds, figuring she's on a roll.

Summer turns her back to Dr. Vic so that only Wilma can see her. She opens her mouth in a hippopotamus-size yawn, and then scratches absently under her bottom lip.

Wilma's hand flies up to cover her mouth.

Psyche.

"Your recall seems very thorough, Ms. Urser," Dr. Vic says. She turns to us. "Who's read Bishop's chart?"

We all have. Dr. Vic should know that. Normally, she *would* know that. It's written in the daily review sheet.

Crack two.

Stress is unwinding her. Bad medicine, especially for a doctor. They have such a high suicide rate. So why would anyone want to be one? Maybe I don't, Ira. No matter what you say. Taking a snow machine into the Brooks Range when it's twenty-five below, surfing in Maui when the waves conspire to kick your butt before board hits the water; high-wire without a net. Really testing the limits.

Now, *that's* living.

"We read about how Bishop has Tourette's syndrome," Becky says. It's her way of telling Dr. Vic we've all read his chart. Trust Becky to opt for kindness rather than going for Wilma's confrontational mode.

We all nod.

"It's good you're all up to speed on this," Dr. Vic says briskly. Which is good, because the assembled masses are figuring out that she knows she's not up to speed. Which is stressing her out even more.

"This is an interesting and complex syndrome. Have any of you ever dealt with it before?"

Wilma's hand flies skyward. "My uncle has a mild case," she says without waiting for Dr. Vic. "But he still functions perfectly well. He's a therapist. Sometimes he brays. That's about it."

Zoey almost snorts out a laugh and has to bite it back.

Dr. Vic nods. "A mild case. Bishop's condition is not mild. Normally, we'd put him in his own room. But the ward's packed, so we've put him with Jerome Franklin. He has excellent coping skills. You've read the chart? Then let's go in and get started."

Get started? Now? What about a review of what Tourette's syndrome is? How it manifests? All the usual stuff.

Zip. Nada. The shortest presentation in history from Dr. Vic. Crack three and you're out.

I look at Zee. She's got her game face on. A quick glance at Summer, who doesn't seem aware that I exist. Focused beyond belief while at work. Standing as far from me during rounds as possible.

Keeping work and play separate.

Dr. Vic leads our merry little band into Jerome's room. Jerome isn't there—probably working the peds floor as usual. Or visiting little Kelly, still recovering from getting her leg crushed in the accident. Jerome's her idol. She tells me she's ready to join his gang.

The one that doesn't really exist.

Bishop Wilson. A beautiful ten-year-old boy, in bed, IV drip in his arm. He could be a movie star. Blond, angelic face, chiseled cheekbones. Looks like an illustration from a Christmas card.

Except that he keeps jerking the arm that doesn't have the IV in it. Then touches his chin. Over and over. And blinking like he's sending Morse Code with his eyes.

My mind reels it off:

Tourette's syndrome is so called because it is diagnosed on the basis of the symptoms it produces, not with a specific diagnostic test. Both motor and vocal tics must be present for the diagnosis of TS to be made, though other symptoms may be present.

Wonder which medical book I read that one in? Wonder why I remember everything I read?

People act as if it's a cute trick like wiggling my ears. They say: What's it like? I think that's like a blind person asking a sighted person what seeing is like.

It just is.

TS is a very, very sucky thing for a kid to have to deal with.

"Good morning, Bishop," Dr. Vic says pleasantly.

"Good morning, Dr. Vic," Bishop says, beaming an angelic smile, accompanied by eye blinks and fearsome twitches. "How are you today?"

"Fine, Bishop, thank you."

Wilma's wide mouth goes into cavernous smile mode. Bishop is such a lovely kid, she's thinking. I hope I have one just like him one day.

Without TS, of course.

"These are the students I told you about," Dr. Vic says, ignoring Bishop's tics.

Bishop repeats, "These are the students I told you about."

Dr. Vic nods. "They'd like to speak with you."

"They'd like to speak with you," whines Bishop.

Echolalia. A TS thing in some people. An uncontrollable urge to repeat what's said to them.

"I like students! I like school!" Bishop yelps. His blinking eyes go from Jerrad to Wilma. "Big mouth! Big mouth!" he cries. His eyes fly over the rest of us, lighting on Becky. "Nice hooters, hooters, hooters! Big mouth, big hooters, big mouth, big hooters!"

Becky maintains somehow, the consummate pro.

Wilma looks like she wants to fall through the floor.

"Dr. Vic, may I ask Bishop a question?" Summer asks.

Dr. Vic nods.

"Bishop, I know it must be difficult sometimes when you find yourself blurting out things that you don't want to say," Summer begins, with the un-Summer earnestness she shows only with kids. "I can tell just by looking at you that you're the kind of person who wouldn't want to hurt anyone's feelings."

Bishop blinks and twitches.

"Is there anything we can do for you while you're here, to make it easier for you when you say things to other kids that you don't mean to say?" Summer asks.

Bishop blinks, twitches, barks. "I like other kids, but they don't like me."

Summer nods sympathetically.

We all do, actually.

"What I like is . . ." Bishop thinks a minute, goes for a couple more barks.

"What I like is to get everything I want, all the time. And hooters!"

6

TRISTAN

"She's runnin' on empty," I tell Chad an hour later as Hirsute and a couple other peds nurses try to quiet the fifteen or twenty kids gathered around a make-shift puppet theater set up in the peds lounge. There's going to be a puppet show, and the kids are excited.

Why shouldn't they be? It's a break from the routine of scary sickness, pain, healing, surviving, dying.

"Who?" Chad asks, absentmindedly.

"Dr. Vic."

"What do you mean?"

"She's still too flipped out over Tia to—"

"Tristan!" a little girl's voice yelps joyfully. It's Kelly, being wheeled in by a nurse's aide. Kelly has a cast on her left leg with pins sticking out of it, from where they did surgery on her after the big accident.

It's not enough that she's got brittle diabetes, I think. Now this, too.

"Hey, how's my girl?" I ask, going to give her a kiss.

"Yo, Tristan!" Jerome's voice booms as he swiftly maneuvers across the lounge on his crutches. "You makin' moves on my woman? I'll get my posse to ice you!"

Kelly giggles, flashing missing front teeth. She adores the linoleum Jerome limps on.

"Hey, man, I never poach on a friend's lady," I tell Jerome. "Ex-specially when she's six."

"Okay, you cool," Jerome decides.

"Will you sign my cast, Tristan?" Kelly asks.

"She only wants da people to sign wid da pink Day-Glo marker," the nurse's aide explains, in a delicious, lilting island accent. Jamaica? She flashes me a similarly delicious island smile. Her skin is melted chocolate. Her neck like a swan's.

She holds out the marker.

I write my name and add a heart.

Jerome sees, frowns. "I don't wanna have to take you outside and jack you up," he tells me.

I nod solemnly, change the heart into a four-leaf clover. Kelly eats this up.

"Thanks, Tristan!" Kelly plants a kiss on my cheek. Nothing like being kissed by a kid. Summer sees, smiles. There's a glorious softness in her incredible eyes when she's on the peds floor.

Sometimes I think: Will the real Summer Everly please stand up?

"If Zoey can get through this with a straight face, we're buying her double mocha javas at Aesop's," Becky whispers to me.

Zee's back behind the puppet show stage, fortunate to have been hand-picked to help with the show by the play therapist, Ms. Bell.

Or, as she's known to patient and staff alike, Tinkerbell.

Jerome claims Tinkerbell is so sweet she gave Kelly diabetes.

"You need anything?" Jerome asks Kelly.

She smiles.

"You be needing anything?" the nurse's aide from the Caribbean asks me pointedly, her voice low.

I smile.

"You think Tinkerbell brought fairy dust?" Matt Everson lisps in a falsetto. He's thirteen, small for his age, a reeper due to a rare bowel disorder. He hides his colostomy bag under huge sweatshirts.

Orlando Ruiz, age twelve and quite the junior stud, makes loud kissing noises. He's on crutches today instead of in his wheelchair, and happy about it. Juvenile rheumatoid arthritis is a nasty and unpredictable disease.

Tinkerbell comes out in front of the puppet stage. She's got a huge pink smiley-face button pinned to her uniform. Her blond hair hangs in two braids.

Tinkerbell meets Heidi.

"Today, boys and girls, we have a really special treat for you," she begins. "We're going to put on a puppet show. How many of you like puppets?"

The little kids all yell "yeah!" but Matt makes a loud gagging noise. Jerome whips out his sunglasses and jams them on his face. His verdict: too weenie for words—he's taking himself out of the action.

"In our puppet show," Tinkerbell simpers, "we're all going to learn about a very, very interesting disorder that one of our new friends here is dealing with."

"Diarrhea!" Orlando calls from behind his cupped hand.

"This disorder is called Tourette's syndrome." Tinkerbell ignores Orlando. "Can you all say Tourette's syndrome?"

The little kids comply, except Kelly. She's copying Jerome's disgust.

And there go a tiny pair of wraparound sunglasses on her eyes. Good one.

"Very good!" Tinkerbell actually applauds. "Just like one of you might have a disorder of your joints, or cancer, or diabetes," (she looks meaningfully at Kelly, who folds her arms like Jerome, air-conditioning personified) "Tourette's syndrome is also a disorder. It is the disorder that Bishop Wilson has. Bishop is Jerome's new roommate."

"Yeah, and he be obnoxious!" Jerome declares.

"Yeah," Kelly agrees with her idol.

Orlando and Matt crack up. We SCRUBS struggle to keep our faces businesslike.

"Now, now, kids, we don't call each other names here, ever," Tinkerbell reminds them. "And when you understand why Bishop is the way he is, you'll see that he can actually be a great friend."

"Not!" Matt hoots.

Tiffany Poe, also thirteen, battling Hepatitis C, self-proclaimed arbiter of cool, snaps at Matt. "Uh, please update your concept of hip expressions. So I don't have to urp."

"Yeah, well, I urp just lookin' at you" is Matt's instant comeback.

"Let's get back to Bishop, shall we?" Tinkerbell asks brightly. "Look at it this way. Each one of us is different and special in our own way. Bishop's way of being different and special is a wonderful chance for us all to learn a wonderful lesson about true friendship."

"Wonderful." Matt scowls.

Tinkerbell scoots back behind the puppet stage, and the littlest kids cheer.

A puppet pops up on the stage. He's brown-skinned and wears a red shirt. "Hi! My name is Juan and I have Tourette's syndrome!" Tinkerbell says. "Oh, look! A new friend is coming to visit me!"

Another puppet appears. Blond, curly-haired, with kewpie-doll lips. "Hi, Juan," says Zoey. "My name is Crystal. Can you explain to me what Tourette's syndrome is?"

It's clear that Zoey is reading from a script. A puppeteer she may not be, but she gives it the ol' Oklahoma try.

Juan tells Crystal that Tourette's syndrome is a brain disorder involving brain chemicals that get very out of whack.

"Sometimes it makes me have tics," Juan explains. "And sometimes it makes me shake or grunt or make some pretty funny noises. Sometimes I say rude things, or even use bad words. And sometimes I repeat what people say and they think I'm making fun of them. But I'm not doing it on purpose!"

"I see," says earnest puppet Crystal in an I'm-reading-from-the-script Zee voice. "So you can't stop it anymore than I can stop . . . breathing?"

"Right!" Juan exclaims. "Just like you can try to stop breathing for a little while by holding your breath, but after a while you just can't help it and you have to breathe again. Well, that's how it is with the stuff that Tourette's syndrome makes me do!"

"Wow," says Crystal. "Did you catch it like I caught the chicken pox once?"

"Nope," Juan replies. "It's not catchy at all. And I need to be able to do my tics and stuff, because if I don't, I can feel really bad. And sad. And that makes it even worse."

"I get it," says Crystal. " 'Cuz you can't help it!"

"I can't help it!" Juan agrees. "Oh, that time I was just agreeing with you, not doing an echo tic!"

Juan and Crystal hug as only puppets can.

"Juan," Crystal says, "I really want you to be my friend."

"I'd love for you to be my friend," Juan says shyly. Then he barks. Like a dog. Literally.

"Oops."

"You don't have to feel bad," Crystal assures him. "It was just Tourette's syndrome that made you bark. Can we be best friends?"

This is the cue for the various nurses and aides to applaud, and they do, shooting us SCRUBS pointed looks.

Yeah, we join right in.

Tepid applause from the little kids.

"No offense, but your play stinks, man," Jerome pronounces.

Matt holds his noise. "Yeah, man, who cut the cheese?"

Tinkerbell and Zoey come out from behind the stage and take a bow. Now everyone really applauds. For Zee, clearly. Hey, the girl hung in there.

Even Summer is clapping for Zoey.

But her hands are hardly touching.

I step out of the cafeteria line holding my tray and look for an empty place to sit in the Effing-Huh cafeteria. But it's feeding time for the circus animals, the noon rush, and hardly a seat is open in the staff area. I spot the SCRUBS minus Summer, but there's no room at their table. I head to the section reserved for the public.

An elderly couple stands up and I settle in. My plan is, eat fast, get outside, maybe jog to the beach and back. It'll help me get through the afternoon. There's a mirrored wall in front of me, and I watch myself taste my coffee—more piss poor than usual—

and bite into a chicken salad sandwich—ditto.

This is not actual food. More like sub-food.

Then, I see something unusual in the mirror in front of me.

Actually, the mirror is reflecting another mirror. It's the oddest thing. I'm getting a top view of a table a hundred yards or more from me, in the administration/staff section of the cafeteria.

Two heads at that table.

Dr. Bradley's bald spot.

And Summer's shining blond glory.

It's her body language that stops me from ingesting the next mouthful of shriveled sandwich. That's no body talking strictly business.

That's something very, very different.

Dr. B says something earnest. He swipes his hand across his face, like he's erasing something. Or suffering something. Then, for the briefest moment, Summer leans in and puts her hand on his white-coated arm. She gets up, walks away.

I go back to my lunch.

Fifty seconds later I catch the faint afterglow of last night's De Rien.

"Howdy, partner."

I turn around. She's gone southern cute on me. Very odd. Very not Summer.

"Hey." I'm eyeing her eyeing me. She picks up my radar. And my radar is saying: What's up with you?

She sits next to me, leans in. "You know what I

was thinking? We don't play enough. Don't you think?"

I spoon a wilted grape. Silent.

"You know Aesop's? On Main Street?"

Sure, I know Aesop's. The only real coffeehouse in Cape Fable, very laid back, sometimes live music at night, though I've never gone to hear it. I've only been there for early morning OJ and coffee after dawn beach patrol.

"Well, Leo is all fired up about this blues band that's playing there tonight. I guess he knows them, and he says they're great. He really wants all of us to meet him and his friends tonight. And you know, he's still going through such a difficult time . . ."

"Is this the new considerate Summer?" I ask.

"Why, Tristan, I happen to be a woman of the utmost consideration," she says flirtatiously. "And I know that although you eschew anything that might smack of mass culture, would you consider being my escort this evening?"

I have no other plans for the evening besides writing e-mail to Stevie and contemplating what in the world I might say to Billie.

And keeping visions of Zee girl out of my head at inappropriate moments.

But before I can say yes, Summer leans even closer and adds, "I'm not planning to wear any panties."

Visions dance in my head. Not of sugarplums.

She drifts off and I glance back into the mirror. Dr. B is gone.

Maybe I imagined the whole thing.

Maybe someone else would believe that. Not me. I saw what I saw what I saw.

"Hey, what's up?" Zoey asks, pulling out the seat that Summer just vacated. Becky leans in over me and plucks an apple slice from my fruit. She holds it up, makes a face. "This smells like sweat socks."

"Hey, listen," Zoey jumps in, "we wanted to invite you to go with us tonight to Aesop's. Leo's friends are playing or something. Anyway, a whole bunch of us are going. You wanna come?"

Zee girl direct but all casual. Hanging with the group, not with her in particular. Crystal clear.

Before I can answer, De Rien floats in.

"Tristy," Summer coos, coming up behind me and Becky, "walk me to the library? I need to take this back."

She holds up the latest issue of the journal *Science*, the one with the article in it about new latest advances in the treatment of myelin destruction in multiple sclerois.

I've read it, too. Which means I can quote it.

"Sure." I turn to Zoey. "Actually, Leo's invite to Aesop's tonight is making the rounds. Summer already invited me."

Summer smiles at Zoey in a manner that could freeze Hirsute's mustache.

"Well," she says to Zee and Becky, "I guess Tristan and I will see you there."

7
ZOEY

Online IRC chat
zthemind@juno.com
mario-ole!@wanadoo.su

Zoey: Hey, Erin the Body, you there?

Erin: Every centimeter of 100% Okie pulchritude. They use centimeters here. What's a centimeter? A meter that smells. Get it?

Z: Too much sex avec Mario a.k.a. Quatro M is rotting your brain. Nice of you to mention that he has an Internet-equipped puter at suisse chalet. We could have been online together a long time ago.

E: Bitch, bitch, bitch. And he's Triple M, you witch. Mini definitely doesn't make the cut.

Z: Is he?

E: Muscles, yes. Boy parts, no. You a doc yet?

Z: Not even close. Why are you still with MAR-RIED Mario? Just another fling?

E: Don't shout. Just haven't flung this one yet. Here's a hint, Okie sistuh. It's good to be rich.

Z: I forget, what's it called when you do it with a guy for money?

E: I forget, what's it called when you don't do it with the guy you want 'cuz you're such a wuss?

Z: Stalemate.

E: Ha. And my dumbass brother told me I was too big of an airhead to play chess. Want to know what I'm wearing right this minute?

Z: Gee, I didn't dress for cyber sex.

E: A diamond necklace from Triple M. Swear to God.

Z: Are you really into him?

E: He's really into me. Get it?

Z: Got it. So I was dumb to worry?

E: Yep.

Z: Why'd he sound so pissed?

E: Short fuse. No prob. 'Zup with the guy you long to de-bone?

Z: I'm wincing. You de-bone fish. Less than zero. Got invited to hang at this coffeehouse tonight. Got up nerve and invited him. Turns out he's already planning to be there. With Triple B HER.

E: Don't shout. Let's kick her ass.

Z: Then he'll just wanna lick her wounds. Puke.

E: Do something to make him jealous. Send a letter to Delia and ask her to move in with you.

Z: You're retrogressing. Besides, you can't make a guy jealous unless he's into you. He isn't into me.

E: No one is into you. Get it?

Z: Stop asking me that. Your jokes suck.

E: And you don't. Which is your prob, Mother Teresa. You radiate touch-me-not vibes of the permanently virginal.

Z: I do not. Do I?

E: Yep. Maybe he thinks you're gay.

Z: And madly in love with you, Okie sistuh. Right.

E: That's Triple M's fantasy. Hop on a plane.

Z: Did someone put Ecstasy in your rum and Coke?

E: Please. Mario and I swill only the best champagne. And the menage thing was a JOKE.

Z: Ha-ha. Don't shout.

E: Unless you're serious.

Z: You're demented. Gotta run, late for Aesop's. Wish you were here sans triple M, Okie sistuh.

E: I never knew you were bilingual.

Z: I'm not. I only like guys. GET IT??

E: !Quippy. Listen, put on something cute for once. Maybe he'll at least realize you're female. Mario awaits nubile me in boudoir. Something about bubble bath, a razor, and heart-shaped pubes.

Z: Gee, thanks for sharing. XXXX Zee-the-Mind

E: Zee?

Z: 'Swhat he calls me.

E: He gave you a PET NAME? Wear something cute, you butthole, and jump him! XXXX EITSAD

Z: EITSAD?

E: Erin-in-the-Sky-Avec-Diamonds

Becky, Chad, and I stroll down the boardwalk toward Aesop's Coffeehouse. Sunset's putting on the glitz, but I barely notice. Neither does Becky or Chad.

She's doing deeply-bummed over hiding love life from The Virus.

He's doing high-anxiety over Secret Admirer mash note he left for Eve.

That's why neither notice that, for the first time since they've known me, I actually show skin. Lace camisole T and skirt. Denim jacket. Mascara and perfume.

The Skank would be so proud.

But my friends do not say jack. Not exactly an ego boost. I was feeling so girly-girl. Must look more like I'm in drag.

Aesop's just up ahead. I check out cleavage. My own. Out there for the world to see. Button jean jacket.

"Leave it open," Becky instructs. "You look so cute."

I cut my eyes at her. "I'm so pathetic that you're throwing me a bone?"

Becky goes hang-dog. "I didn't even tell you how cute you look, did I?" Nudges Chad. "Did you tell her how cute she looks?"

"Yeah," Chad asserts. "Didn't I?"

"No and it's no biggie, okay?" I lie. "It's just, you know, I usually wear baggy stuff."

"Hey, that's right," Chad says. Divine revelation.

Becky throws an arm around my shoulders. "Don't take that personally. Chad's only got eyes for Eve. Gwyneth, Jennifer Love, and Angelina Jolie could strip in front of the man and beg for it—all at the same time, mind you. He wouldn't see 'em."

Chad: "I'd see 'em. I just wouldn't be interested."

Becky looks utterly skeptical. "This Eve chick deserves such undying devotion?"

"She's amazing," Chad asserts. "If you knew her, you'd understand." Then he starts to whistle. Wheels turn visibly in his transparent little mind. "Hey, I just thought of a great idea!"

"What?" I'm deeply dubious.

"You two should get to know Eve!"

Huh?

"Isn't that a great idea?"

I get it. Me to Becky: "I'm guessing that translates to: 'suss the girl out and report back to Secret Admirer who won't sign his name at the bottom of a love note."

"Does it?" Becky asks him.

"Kinda," Chad admits sheepishly. "What, bad idea?"

"Real," say I. "You're no geek, Chad. Not anymore. I'm sure Eve would love to see you again."

Yeah. Me giving guy advice.

"Great. I'll be sure to do that . . . after you find out if she's dating anyone."

Shameless begging gesture follows.

I shake my head. "Sorry. I suck at subterfuge."

"Bull," Becky says, laughing. "Who'd you wear that sexy little cammie for tonight, Miss Subterfuge Queen?"

"What do you mean?" squeaks a voice that knows exactly what Becky means.

The voice sounds a lot like mine.

"You're busted." Becky laughs again and hugs me. Fortunately Chad is too involved in latest Eve fantasy to track this.

We hit Aesop's. Across the boardwalk from the beach. Weathered wood. Mismatched chairs torn from a torn-down theater. Hipper-than-thou staff. Outdoor-indoor small stage, smaller dance floor.

Beyond packed. Hot local blues band Smells Like Tuna wails the blues.

Way Effing-Huh! happening place.

Smells Like Tuna got their start at Aesop's, just got a record deal. The townies are going wild. Heat to the beat. Bodies everywhere. Lights dance on the lead singer. He's sizzling. Everything's sizzling.

"I wish Rick was here!" Becky yells into my ear. I nod and look empathetic, trying not to bird-dog for Tristan and Female Perfection in obvious fashion.

"C'mon, let's get nasty!" Becky pulls me and Chad into gyrating mass of bodies.

That Becky can dance doesn't surprise me. But Chad? Prep puppy goes hound dawg dirty. Subtle. Teasing. Laid back. Hot.

Like, there's more where this came from.

Yowza.

"Where did you learn to dance like that?" Becky yelps.

Chad grins. "Chi-towners grow up on the Bulls and the blues. Makes us wanna dance!"

The lead singer moans into the mic:

My baby was a hoochie momma
Spend my pay and lay about.
Say my baby was a hoochie momma
You know I shoulda turned her out.
But every time she makes me holler
You know I got to scream and shout.

Just like that! Do it just like that!
You know it keeps me comin' back
Just like that.

Townies go to town on the chorus of "Just Like That." Soon we do, too.

Just like that.

Someone taps me on the shoulder. I spin.

"Zee girl," Someone says.

God, Someone's handsome.

What say we go get naked and you lick the back of my knees? suggests wanton Zoey. Read: only in my mind, per usual.

Wuss Zoey just smiles. He volleys it back.

Meaningfully? Or wishful thinking?

I hear Erin's voice in my head: *Okie Sistuh, kindly get it through your head that you are a stone vixen sometime before middle-age spread kicks in.*

Vixen Zoey in strappy cammie sings "Just like that!"

At Tristan.

Not just in my mind, either.

I'm dancing. Nice and slow. Like there's more where this came from. From across the Atlantic, I'm channeling Erin's nerve.

I lift my arms. Reach for Tristan's neck. He's smiling. Meaningfully, I swear it. Just like that, and—

Oh, God.

He's smiling at Summer. Not me. She approaches from behind me. Slips into his arms. *Molds* herself to him.

"Hey," she purrs.

"Hey! Hi! Wow, fun in here, huh?" jumps out of my mouth. Loud. Manic.

Like she was saying "hey" to me.

Like anyone believes that.

Like I am the brasshole of the new millennium.

"Why, Zoey," Summer says, her chin against Tristan's clavicle. "Do you have on mascara? You do. That's so sweet! I told you if you made a little effort it would help. Got a hot date, or just lookin' to get lucky?"

No, itching to put my fist through your Triple B smirk, think I, queen of unarticulated comebacks.

I mumble inaudibly.

Summer is It. Every intimidating Triple B, times infinity.

And she knows it.

I back away. "Well, I—"

"Zee—" Tristan begins as someone else says "Zoey!" like seeing me is a happy surprise.

My butt backs into steel. No, muscle.

Zen Greg.

"Great to see you!" Zen bellows over the blues.

"Oh, wow, you too!" Throw arms around Zen G

for enthusiastic hug. For benefit of Tristan and Summer.

Zen G assumes he just got lucky.

He takes my hand to lead me away. I go girly-girl, waggle fingers preciously at Tristan and *her*. I'm led through the crowd to massive table outside.

"Hey, look who I found," he tells Leo, the NicoTwins, assorted others. Leo hugs me like a long, lost friend. Others offer raucous greetings.

"Hey, remember me? From the beach? Tisha? And this is Allie?"

NicoDaisy Tisha works it in cheek-peek cut-offs and belly baring T. NicoDots Allie tones it down in drawstrings and oversized Fable Harbor High baseball jersey.

Twin Marlboros burning in the ashtray on the table, I assure the NicoTwins I remember them.

"Hey, Zoey, you ever had an Icy Fiend?" Zen G asks.

He lifts a tall frosted glass to my lips. I sip.

"Now, that's strong," I manage.

"Triple iced espresso with crushed espresso ice, cherry juice, and espresso whipped cream," Zen G explains. "Want one?"

Wild Zoey. "Sure."

"Be right back." Zen G hustles off to get my caffeine buzz.

Tisha hands me her glass, picks up burning Marlboro in an unmanicured hand. "Mine's better. Taste."

I do. Choke. Everyone laughs. The alcohol they

don't serve at Aesop's has migrated into Tisha's drink.

" 'S' called a Hot Icy Fiend," Tisha explains. "Way better." She takes massive glug. "Hey, is that friend of yours here?"

"She means Tristan," Leo fills in, bopping to the beat.

Like I didn't know.

"Yeah," I say.

"Yeah?" Tisha shakes limp hair off face. Downs fifty percent of Hot Icy Fiend. "So, are you two, like, a thing?"

"Good question," says Zen G, quickly back with my liquid buzz in event Tristan were to drift over in his absence.

I utter three most vacant words in history of English language, both written and spoken.

"We're just friends."

"Good." Zen G smiles at me. Sits.

"Ooh, Greg hears the boo-tay call of lo-o-ve!" NicoDaisy Tisha coos, cracking herself up. Imbibes more Hot Icy Fiend.

"You might wanna chill on that," Greg suggests.

Tisha downs the rest of her drink. Fat Adam Sandler hands her another. She sucks it up.

"That's, um, like your third one," Allie points out timidly. Stubs out cigarette. Lights another.

"Bummer," says Tisha. "I should be way beyond three by now."

"Par-tay!" Leo whoops, twirling his fist in the air.

Tastes Like Tuna launches into kickin' groove. Tisha closes eyes and sings along.

Correction. Slurs along.

Zen G leans in close. "She's a nice kid, but she gets a little out of control. Her older brother's a friend of mine. Got some insane bug up his ass and joined the Air Force. I try to look after her for him."

I smile. Like I care.

"Listen, I want to make sure she gets home okay," Zen goes on. "So I could take her on my Harley. But I'm kind of hoping I'll be finding her another ride, 'cuz I'll be taking you."

I'm saved by Becky, Chad, Summer, and Tristan, all arriving at once. Leo goes berserk with joy, pushes chairs around to make room, yells intros over the music no one can hear.

"You didn't have to leave," Becky says in my ear. "I can't believe you let Summer intimidate you like that."

My response: meaningful eye rolls, as Zen talks with Leo. Looks over his massive shoulder at me. Smiles.

End of eye rolls.

"Who's Mr. Clean?" Becky asks.

I yell his name at her.

"He's cute," she says. "Testosterone definitely dancing in your direction."

Chad asks Becky to dance. They head inside.

"Hey, surf guy, what's happening?" NicoTwin Daisy shouts to Tristan across the table.

He shrugs.

"You remember me? Tisha? From the beach?"

He nods.

Tisha lights a ciggie off Fat Adam. Sucks up rest of Hot Ice Fiend. Eyes Summer. "Who're you?"

"Sylvia Plath," Summer replies sweetly.

"Yeah?" Tisha exhales. "So, Sylvia, you and Tristan got it going on or what?"

Well, well. Let's sit back and watch Summer's claws come out. At someone else, for once.

"Oh, no, he's my brother," Summer explains.

Say what?

Tristan looks bemused.

Tisha's eyes go scrunchie. She's on her feet and wobbling close to Summer. "Yeah, you guys look kinda alike." She sniffs.

"You're wearing that perfume that Cameron Diaz wears, right? Expensive French stuff?"

"De Rien," Summer utters.

"Yeow." Tisha steps backward, waves her hand in front of her face. "I'm allergic. Gives me nasty hives like I got scabies or something. 'Member, Allie?"

Allie nods. "We tried samples at the mall. Tish got all these bumps."

"Maybe it was something you ate. I doubt it was from perfume that costs two hundred an ounce," Summer says sweetly.

Tisha lurches forward, rubs her arm on Summer. "You'll see. Oh, man, I love this song!" Ciggie falls from lower lip as she jumps onto the table and gyrates like a cage dancer at Café au Laid.

Cheek-peek shorts provide interesting anatomical view. Many men viewing.

"You got it goin' on, baby!" yells Fat Adam.

"Not even," I mutter.

Zen reaches for Tisha's purse. Pulls out a pint of Jack. Pockets it.

Tisha's rolling—actually, her pelvis is rolling—for Tristan. Gyrating. Hands over head. Her navel ring looks infected. No. It's hives. Two hundred dollar an ounce perfume hives. Take that, Female Perfection.

NicoTwin Tisha checks Tristan for horn dog reaction.

Zip.

So it's time for serious down and dirty. Commence lap dancing hives display.

"How sweet, brother dearest, she's dancin' for you," Summer drawls.

Tisha says she just feels the music. Right. On Tristan's lap. Licks her lips. Shakes all shakeable parts in brother dearest's face.

Sister dearest Sylvia eggs Tisha on. Tisha sucks up eggs and cranks it to eleven.

Bizarre.

Then a light dawns. Summer's shining Tisha on 'cuz Tisha's no comp. Whereas I am . . .

Right.

"Hey!" Tisha tries to pull Tristan onto Aesop's table.

Chivalry happens. He stands, takes her hand, dances with her.

Kinda. Tisha's a cat and Tristan's the scratching post. Front and back.

Over Tisha's shoulder, Tristan's eyes are on me. I feel Zen's hand on my shoulder. "Doin' okay?"

"Great."

Tristan's eyes don't move. So I take Zen G's hand.

"Ever rode a Harley?" he asks me.

Me and Tristan: eyelock. To Zen: I shake my head no.

Zen G gently turns me to him. "Will your friend be cool with Tisha? 'Cause she's only eighteen. A real young eighteen."

"Trust me, he won't touch her."

I think: he'll be much too busy getting down and dirty with his sister the dead tormented poet. Tisha is so no comp. She's just a punch line to their private joke.

I glance back at NicoTwin Daisy. She's way, way past trying too hard, now in Tisha Zone of Beyond Pathetic.

"Why, brother dearest, isn't Tisha a wonderful dancer?" Summer asks. "How do you get your breasts to shake like that, honey?"

Tisha demonstrates proudly.

"Hey, Tish, want some plain coffee?" Allie asks.

"I'll get it for you," gallant Tristan offers.

"Coffee's not what I want," Tisha tells him. "Ooo-wee! I'm hotter than a pistol!"

She stumbles. Tristan catches her. Zen G is there in a flash, too.

"Easy does it," Zen tells her, gently leading her to a seat. "Looks like it's crash time for you, little girl."

Tisha cusses him out like a sailor. Her hives stand up and say hey on her butt cheeks.

Allie has returned with Chad. "I hate it when she does this," she says.

"Lighten up," Tisha slurs, weaving.

"No sweat, man, I got her," Fat Adam Sandler says. Tisha ends up over his shoulder, dangling like an accessory scarf.

"Hey," she objects. "Where's the hottie? Surf boy!"

"You cool, Barry?" Zen G asks Fat Adam.

He nods. "Got it covered. You comin', Allie?"

Allie hurries after them. Tisha pounds on Barry a.k.a. Fat Adam Sandler's back, shrieking anatomically impossible if conceptually interesting curses.

"Sorry," Allie calls back at us.

"Cute trio," Summer quips.

"You think those girls are safe with that guy?" Chad the Good asks.

Zen G grins. "Oh, yeah. Barry's a great guy. And he's also gay."

"Nah, man, he's celibate. He used to be bi," Leo insists.

Heated debate between remaining townies ensues. Subject: Barry's sexuality. Or lack thereof. Chad and Becky head for dance floor.

Leaving me. Tristan. Summer. Cute trio.

"Tristan, did you notice how cute our little Zoey looks tonight?" Summer asks.

"Yeah, actually, I did."

"See, Zoey?" Summer says. "It worked. I mean, it is Tristan you wore that little cammie for, isn't it?"

"Not hardly."

"Not hardly," Tristan echoes.

Summer's eyes go wide. "But it's so sweet. You don't need to deny it."

"Just call me Sylvia," say I.

Smells like Tuna segues into a cover of Dylan's "Just Like a Woman." Wordlessly Summer gets up, beckons to Tristan in a way no male could resist.

He doesn't. She melts into his arms. Perfection.

"Trist," I hear her murmur. Then she whispers in his ear. His eyes close. He's lost in her. I can tell.

Zen G leaves debate, comes over to me.

"Can I persuade you to take a ride on my Harley?"

Tristan's eyes open. He's looking at me. Over the perfect shoulder of perfect Summer in his arms.

"Hell, yes," I tell Zen G.

And then I pull all the massive muscles that is Zen G to me.

And I kiss him. Hard and hot.

While Tristan watches.

Kiss finally ends. Tristan's eyes still on me.

"Like a brother," I mouth softly to him.

"A brother," he repeats.

Echolalia.

It's a Tourette's moment.

8
TRISTAN

MEMO
From: DR. VIVIAN PACE
To: ALL SCRUBS

Effective immediately, all SCRUBS are required to spend Saturday morning intensives in the FHUH department assigned to them. The assignment list will be posted on the bulletin board. Initial your assignment by noon each Friday. A concise and detailed written report on the assignment is required and is to be in my box on the following Monday of each week by nine o'clock a.m. Failure to follow your assignment or to turn in your written report will be grounds for immediate dismissal from this program.

Trust The Virus to find a way to pile on the stress load. No more Saturday mornings for surfing or fishing, or to extend Friday night Summer heat into Saturday morning reheat.

Last night at Aesop's, Chad informed me that I'd have the suite all to myself. All night. He gave no details and I asked no questions. Summer and I could leave behind the moonlight and the sand for clean sheets and soft music. Passion in the dunes appeals, but Summer archly explains that women find sand anatomically more challenging than men.

We shower together and I watch as she dresses for Virus-assigned Saturday morning in geriatrics.

Black silk thong panties whisper against her flesh as she pulls them on. She is poetry. Fire and ice.

Last night she was incendiary.

Watching Zoey kissing muscle man was like a fist in my gut. Ask not for whom she's worn the sexy little top, she has not worn it for thee. She said as much, and Zee girl reeks of honesty.

"My brother."

You can't get much clearer than that.

But later—in my bed, on the floor, in the shower, against the wall, Summer took the arts of passion to new heights.

As if she had something to prove.

She fits tiny pearls into her ears, assesses her perfection in the mirror, then turns to me, ready to go.

The image of her in the cafeteria with Dr. B flashes in my mind. Summer leaning toward him.

Her hand on his arm.

"What?" she asks me. "You're staring."

"It's funny," I say. "I know everything about you. And nothing about you."

The smallest smile plays at her lips. "Don't fool yourself, Tristan. That's the way you like it."

I'm assigned to peds. So is Zee. When I get there, she's observing Hirsute set up an IV for a new admit. A girl. Bone-thin. Zee's eyes flick to me, then back to Hirsute. Clearly her interest is less than zero.

"Hey, what's kickin', chicken?" the skinny girl getting her arm punctured asks me.

"Not much," I reply. "I'm Tristan."

"Om," she says, pointing to herself. "Hippie parents. It's a long, sad story. You a doctor?"

"Nope. You?"

Her grin lights up the room. "I like you."

She's tiny, can't be more than ten. Her voice is strangled and raspy. Her shoulders look overdeveloped, as if she's a gymnast. Her fingers are splayed, bulbous above the third joint.

Suddenly she coughs. And can't stop. Deep, hacking, choking coughs.

Silently Hirsute rubs her back.

Cystic fibrosis, I realize. Maybe she's a candidate for a lung tissue transplant and she'll live. Maybe she'll bust an artery, die choking on her own blood.

Om inhales raggedly, gasping for air that can barely find its way in to her phlegmy lungs. Hirsute calmly reaches for the oxygen mask and puts it on her face.

Zoey pales but keeps her face impassive. Her eyes tell the tale, though. She bleeds. The ghost of days past makes a quick reappearance.

"Better?" Hirsute asks when the coughing subsides.

Om nods yes. The oxygen is removed. Hirsute tapes the IV needle in place. "Okay?" she asks.

"You're the best, 'Suit," Om says, breathless but game. "The ouchless wonder. I was afraid I might get stuck with the no-brainer again. My blood's spurting all over the room and she's like, 'Oh, duh! Guess I hit an artery!' "

Hirsute, woman of few words, nods and lumbers out with her blood tray.

"Catch you later," I call to Om as Zoey and I follow Hirsute out of the room.

"Yeah, cool," she calls after me. "Hey, thanks, 'Suit!"

"Does she get admitted a lot?" Zoey asks Hirsute at the nurse's desk.

Hirsute nods but doesn't elaborate. "Dr. Martinez is on call this morning. He wants the two of you to observe in 502."

"Jerome's room," Zoey says.

"He's in P.T. Bishop's in there with his Tourette's support team. They're expecting you."

"What about his FOUO?" Zoey asks. "I mean, that's why he's here."

Hirsute writes something in a file. "Tests. Process of elimination. Between you and me, they're in no hurry. They're too ga-ga over his TS. Dr. Simon's doing a massive TS study. Bishop is a level five."

"Which means?" Zoey ask.

I know.

"One is mild," Hirsute explains. "The highest level Simon and his team have done a work-up on so far is a four, which is quite serious. Level five is sort of off the Richter scale. And Bishop's mom doesn't believe in medicating TS. Bishop Wilson being here means Simon gets to study him at length, which means Simon gets published, big-time, which means more funding for Simon's lab. Welcome to the wonderful world of medicine."

Zoey looks less than psyched. Whether it's from Hirsute laying out the suits on the table or just being in peds, I don't know.

Oh, that nasty little Virus. Summer, who adores children, is stuck in geriatrics. Chad, who'd love to be with the orthopods, is trailing a proctologist. Becky was assigned to Dr. Cool himself, meaning she's going to have to observe Cool examine Rick, the love of her life. Only she can't cop to that. She has to take in Dr. Cool's matter-of-fact report on how much time Rick can last until—unless—a compatible heart and lungs becomes available.

The Virus put each of us where we would least like to be.

Where does that leave me?

Where I would least like to be on a Saturday morning: anywhere inside Effing-Huh.

Zee and I head for 502. The peds floor is busy. Lots of visitors. From one of the rooms come the strains of a bunch of people singing "Happy Birthday" to someone named Aunt Betty.

"Cystic fibrosis," Zoey says, shaking her head. "Now, that's a sucky disease."

"All kids sick enough to end up here have something sucky," say I. "However, some are more sucky than others."

We round the corner, dodge a man carrying a bouquet of GET WELL balloons.

"Have fun last night?" I ask Zee.

"Yeah."

"Greg—that's his name, right? Seems nice."

"How would you know? You didn't say two words to him."

"He was pretty busy," I point out.

Touching you. Kissing you. A bald biker EMT, Zoey? That's what you want?

"So, did you have fun?" she throws back. "You and your sister, Sylvia Plath?" She could have at least picked Elizabeth Barrett Browning.

"Summer was—"

"I don't care what Summer was, is, or will be, okay?"

"Okay."

We walk briskly down the hall.

"Look, we all happened to end up at the same club last night," Zoey goes on. "Summer got off on feeling superior to the townie girls. And you got off on Summer. I'm sure you both had a really swell time."

She's starting to irk me, something she does very well.

So I say, "As indoor activities go, it ranked passably."

I'm graced with an arch Zee girl look. "I'm sure certain indoor activities rank more than *passably* with you, Tristan. Oh, wait! That's right, you prefer sand with your sex."

We're right outside Jerome and Bishop's room. Zoey's face goes all blotchy. Her body tenses.

"Hypothetically, I mean," she adds.

She's lying. I can tell.

Did Summer tell her that we heat up the dunes nearly every night? Are you kidding? Summer confides in no one, least of all Zoey.

Which leaves option number two.

She saw us.

"Zoey—"

She darts into the room, leaving me there. Huh. Tuck that away and contemplate it later.

Angelic-looking Bishop sits on the edge of his bed in full eye-tic, arm-tick mode. He's wearing pajama bottoms and nothing else. And he's singing.

He's singing "The Song That Never Ends." It just goes on and on, my friend.

This is the song that never ends.
It just goes on and on my friend. . . .

Standing around the bed, in full observation mode, are four white-coats. Two men: one tall and bearded, one short with ebony skin and thick glasses Two women: one pear-shaped and nervous, with fingernails bitten to the quick, and the hostess with the mostest, Tinkerbell.

Bishop quits singing and regards us, smiling. "Oh, hi. I remember you guys. How are you today?"

"Fine," Zoey says. "How about you?"

"I still have a fever. And my throat kinda hurts."

Zoey nods. "I'm sorry to hear that."

Bishop shrugs good-naturedly. Blinks. Tics. "Oh, well. Hell. Smell. You smell! You smell! You use hair gel! You smell!"

"Zoey, Tristan!" Tinkerbell greets us like favorite guests at her garden party. "Doctors, these are two of the young people in our SCRUBS program."

She introduces the white coats to us. Dr. Angler, the Abe Lincoln look-alike, is a neuropsychiatrist. Dr. Simon from Botswana is a research scientist doing a study on Tourette's. The nervous, pair-shaped woman is a child psychologist, Dr. Klein.

And Tink is, well . . . Tink.

"Would you like to get dressed today, Bishop?" asks Tinkerbell, in her pretty-please-with-a-cherry-on-top voice.

"Would you like to get dressed today, Bishop?" he echoes.

Tinkerbell holds up a green T-shirt. "How about a nice green—"

"No-o-o-o-o!" Bishop screams. "Hate green, hate green, hate green!"

"Most interesting," Dr. Simon mutters. "Fascinating."

"You're black," Bishop tells Dr. Simon. "Black, hack, sack, rack!"

"A rhyming obsessive-compulsion," Dr. Simon notes eagerly.

"I'm so sorry I said gr—that color you don't like, Bishop," Tink says gravely. "I won't even bring up that color again, because it makes you uncomfortable."

"Right, stupid skinny stick," Bishop says. "You make me sick, ick, ick!"

Dr. Angler nods. "That's okay, Bishop. It's your Tourette's speaking, and you are not your Tourette's."

Tic, tic, snort.

"No," Bishop finally agrees.

Dr. Angler beams at his own success.

"You know, Bishop, it's very important that when Tourette's makes you feel the need to say or do something, that you give yourself permission to do it," Dr. Klein says, not to be outdone by her colleague. "As long as you don't hurt yourself or others."

Snort. Tick.

This is the song that never ends.

Bishop nods as he sings. The med team nods, one big happy nodding family.

"Well, Bishop, we don't want you getting all chilled without a shirt on," Tinkerbell chirps. "So what color T-shirt do you—"

"One moment, please," Dr. Klein interrupts. "Bishop, I care—we all care *very much* about your feelings. How does it make you *feel* when Ms. Bell asks you if you want to wear green?"

She said the G word to test Bishop's reaction, is my guess. He's their guinea pig.

They disgust me.

The team awaits Bishop's answer like it's the Holy Grail. Bishop blinks. Throws in a shoulder tic. Then he leans over and honks Dr. Klein's left breast. "Nice hooters! Nice hooters! Nice hooters!"

Dr. Klein grabs her own chest in protective custody. The others clear their throats and reel off scientific pseudo-guesses about Bishop's obsessive-compulsive impulse to grab the female breast.

Out of the corner of my eye, I notice that Zoey has turned around as if to look at something.

But actually she's silently cracking up.

I love her for that.

"Aw, man, what is *up* with this?"

It's Jerome, limping into his room, Discman blaring some gangsta thing into his ears. All bop and attitude.

My man.

Zoey hugs him. "Hey, Jerome."

"The fine ladies can't keep their hands off me," Jerome says with a fatalistic shrug, snapping off his music.

"Look, Bishop, it's your friend Jerome, back from physical therapy," Tink chirps.

"Hi, Jerome." Bishop grins, eager and friendly.

Jerome shoots him the evil eye and sits on his bed, arms folded, oozing unfriendliness. He uses the remote to click on the overhead TV.

It's a music video and the little words say it's by someone named Wet Tee.

"No, no, no, no!" Bishop yells.

"What is it, the TV?" Dr. Klein asks, hovering.

"I hate that song! Wrong song, wrong song! This is the song that never ends, it just goes on and on my friend, if you want to know . . ."

Tinkerbell smiles at Jerome as Bishop keeps singing. "Might Bishop have a turn with the remote to pick out what he'd like to watch?"

Jerome scowls. "Whatchoo mean, *'a turn'*? Dude thinks it's always his turn, you know what I'm sayin'?"

"Right!" Bishop agrees happily. "Right, bite, tight!"

"You see, Jerome, it's a part of Bishop's TS that makes it difficult for him to share and wait his turn," Dr. Angler explains like he's talking to a two-year-old. "This part of TS is called A.D.D., which stands for—"

"Attention deficit disorder," Jerome fills in. "Neurological disorder of the brain caused by some kinda chemical imbalance. I'm black, not stupid, fool."

Now Zoey is actually biting her lip to keep from laughing out loud. Tears of mirth form in the corners of her eyes.

Bishop screams, "My turn! My turn! My turn!"

Jerome flips him the remote. The white coats breathe a sigh of relief in tandem. Bishop switches channels until he gets to a *Baywatch* repeat. "Nice hooters!"

"Shut up," Jerome snaps.

"Now, Jerome," Dr. Klein chides him. "How do we deal with anger?"

"What's up with that 'we' thang? I get fierce—you don't wanna mess with me. You bite your fingernails."

Jerome pulls out a Gameboy and flicks it on.

"Me, me, me, me!"

Even Tinkerbell seems to wilt around the edges. Yet she presses on. "Maybe after you choose a T-shirt, Jerome will let you have a turn with his—"

"Now, cow! Now, cow! No hooters on the now cow! Now, now, now, now—"

Dr. Simon is scribbling furiously in his notebook.

"Jerome, could Bishop borrow your—" Dr. Klein begins.

"Now-now-now-now!" Bishop is off the bed, twirling, ticking and shrieking "now" at the top of his lungs.

Jerome heaves the Gameboy at him. Bishop reaches and makes a spectacular one-handed grab. Maybe the kid should consider becoming an ice hockey goalie.

"That was nice of you, Jerome," Tinkerbell says.

"Shee—I only did it to shut him up. Hey, I got a question for the brain trust."

"Of course, Jerome," says Dr. Angler.

He hitches his chin toward Bishop. "Ever since he been here, that dude get treated like his don't stink. 'Cuz he got TS. Like we all gotta understand he can't wait his turn, or it's not his fault when he messes up Kelly's coloring book, or whatever."

"Um-hum," Dr. Angler murmurs.

"So, how you know it always his TS make him do it? Like, okay, sometimes TS make him do and say stuff, right? But other times, he do it 'cuz it's how he gets his own way. What if he got you all psyched out, and he just obnoxious?"

The room is strangely silent, except for the voice of Pamela Anderson breathily crying "He's drowning, I'll save him!" on the TV. Bishop has managed to put on a white T-shirt by himself while no one was watching.

He's not singing, I notice.

The white coats finally mumble that it's very complex and they'll be happy to explain more to Jerome later, and they'll be back in a while. They troop out of the room.

Chad's running in. He practically collides with Dr. Klein's recently honked hooters, excuses himself, dodges past and into the room. Bishop pushes buttons on Jerome's Gameboy. Except for the eye-blinking, he's quiet.

"Zup?" Jerome calls to Chad.

"Hey, Jerome, know what I just heard from Lark?" Chad asks. "You worked with a new physical therapist today."

Jerome nods his confirmation. "She was sweet, too."

"Yeah, really?" Chad asks, very hyper.

"You buggin', man," Jerome says. "You do too much caffeine, or what?"

"So, what was this therapist's name?" Chad asks.

Ah. Zoey and I exchange looks. The obvious is coming.

"Eve," says Jerome.

"Eve Carrier?" It comes from Chad's mouth like a prayer.

"Yeah, that's it. She fine, bro. We chillin' back at the movie in the peds lounge tonight."

Chad can hardly breathe. "She'll be there? At the *movie* in the *peds* lounge?"

Jerome grins. "It's a date with fate an' she can't wait. That remind me. I gotta stop at the drugstore."

"Could I come, too?" Bishop asks.

"I can't stop you," Jerome acknowledges.

Chad's fingers rake nervously through his hair. "So, Jerome, what time are you meeting—"

"Jerome, you left this down in P.T.," says a soft voice from the doorway. Dirty blond hair, slender, fresh-faced. The kind of beauty that whispers, lost in a crowd.

Eve Carrier.

No doubt.

And Chad has nowhere to hide.

9
ZOEY

In the flesh. Chad's Dulcinea. A.k.a. Eve Carrier.

Cervantes's heroine? Un-uh. More like Jewel sans guitar and confidence. No. Glinda the Good Witch sans wand and crown.

"Hi, I'm Eve Carrier, one of the physical therapists."

Moment of truth. Intros must happen.

My eyes slide toward Chad Quixote de la Mancha. So do Tristan's.

Chad Q has gone faceless behind his clipboard.

Names are traded. If Glinda recognizes Chad Q, she isn't saying. Meanwhile, Chad Q, in the guise of a walking clipboard, sidesteps toward the door.

Eve to Chad Q: "Are you okay?"

Chad Q to Eve: "Just fine. Gotta run on to an emergency, honey." Chad Q with an Elvis-sounding voice disappears out the door.

Tristan. I notice every little thing about him. Like how he has one dimple. Which surfaces only during suppressed laughter.

Which surfaces now.

"Who was that?" Airy Eve asks.

Uh . . .

We're saved by Jerome, who's hooting. "Man, he buggin'!"

Echolalic Bishop: "Man, he buggin'!"

"Shut up, fool," Jerome snaps. "And gimme back my Gameboy."

"Buggin'! Huggin'! Fuggin'!" Bishop holds the Gameboy tight to his chest. Tics on a rampage. Blinks. Throws in a few barks for good measure.

Glinda the Good focuses on Bishop, Chad Q now out of sight, out of mind. She floats toward Bishop in ethereal Good-Witch-Earth-Mother-Woodstock-Granola-Crunchie-Wannabe fashion.

Inner-bitch begs me to hum "Puff, the Magic Dragon." I struggle. Resist.

"Hello," from Glinda the Good.

"Hello. My name is Bishop. How are you?"

"Actually, I was really upset this morning. My cat Julius got sick last night, and I was really worried about him—he's nineteen, and I've had him since he was six weeks old. So I took him to the vet. She said it isn't serious, so I feel a lot better now."

Note to self: a) Scratch the Glinda Good Witch thing. Because b) Eve is for real and c) this is first time someone actually answers Bishop's "how are you?" instead of d) just saying "fine" and e) less attention to my burgeoning inner-bitch is deeply warranted.

Bishop glows. Softly says, "I'm glad."

"Maybe sometime you'll come down to PT with Jerome," Eve offers. "There's a lot of stuff we can do—"

"Yeah!" Bishop cries.

"You ain't seein' my woman on my time, fool."

Eve nods. "I see your point."

Jerome does badass gangsta head-bob thing. "Damn straight."

Eve tells Bishop she'll see what she can work out, and he nods.

The ticking beast has been tamed. Temporarily.

"Nice to meet you all," Eve says, heading for the door. "I'll see you tonight, Jerome."

"Sublime, divine, and right on time," Jerome calls after her.

"Sublime, divine, and right on time," Bishop echoes.

Jerome's hands fly north. "You see? He normal when he wanna be. Wha'choo wanna bet he be psyching out the brain trust all along?"

"Along! Gong! Wrong! *Song*!" Bishop launches into his favorite melody:

> *"This is the song that never e-e-e-e-nds!*
> *It just goes on and on my fri-e-e-e-e-nd!"*

"I'm through messin' with you!" Jerome yells over Bishop's serenade.

"Listen, you two—" I interject. Pathetically. Look to Tristan for reinforcement. He's elsewhere.

So annoying. *So* Tristan.

> *"If you want to know who started it,*
> *Well, no one really knows . . ."*

This time it's Jerome warbling, vocal chords in the key of earsplit.

"You got a five-count to give up my Gameboy!" he stops his song to shout. "And one through four already happened *mentally*, you know what I'm sayin'? *Four and a half . . .*"

> *"This is the song that never en-n-n-ds!*
> *It just goes on and on, my fri-e-e-e-n-d!"*

Mea culpa. I am unworthy of a career in medicine. Read: I want to kill the kid.

"You guys surf much?" Tristan asks. Laid back. Easy. Like their out-of-control has no control over his control.

Unlike me.

Schlitz.

Instant silence.

Ahhh. They regard him.

I aim for mental picture of small black kid with one leg and smaller white kid with involuntary body tics riding longboards side by side.

Fail miserably.

"Brothers don't surf," Jerome scoffs. "Surfin' be *white*, man."

Like lack of second leg on which to balance has nothing to do with it.

"I'm white," Bishop offers.

Jerome snorts, "You got that right, Caspar."

Feeling overmatched in coping department, I throw in, "There are surfers of every color."

"Yeah?" Jerome's face goes sly. "Black? White? Yellow? Brown? How about . . . *GREEN*?"

"Hate-green hate-green hate-green!" Bishop wails.

Jerome scores himself one point in the air.

Tristan leans against the wall, triple blasé. "There are champion surfers with one leg, too."

Jerome eyes him warily. "For real?"

"For real."

"For real!" Bishop yells. "Real, deal, steal—"

Jerome claps his hands over his ears. "That's it. Me and my homies gots to take this boy *out*—"

"First surfing lesson," Tristan goes on, like this is a normal conversation, "is to listen to yourself." He taps his temple. "Here."

The Boyz in the Hood consider this. Baby blue eyes blink rapidly. Brilliant black eyes say Tristan, bro', you full of schlitz.

But Tristan talks the talk. *And* walks the walk. Kids suss this stuff out. He the man, The Boyz listen.

Soon they're standing in the center of their beds. Eyes closed. Arms extended. Balancing. Listening. In *here*.

Bishop tics. But he's silent. Amazing.

"Bishop, baby!"

The spell is broken as Bishop's mother races across the room. An Erin special Triple N neo NASCAR nymphette rode hard and put up wet. Too much: cleavage, perm, worry. Too little: education, money, luck.

Thirty going on forty-five.

"Hi, Mom. How are you?" Bishop asks.

"Fine, baby. I'm supposed to be meeting Dr. Vic here." She pushes golden hair off his forehead, frowns. "You still got fever. What the hell are they doing in this place?"

"Hey, guess what, Mom? Tristan's teaching me and Jerome how to surf!"

She cranes around, eyes Tristan, all tough-chick who-the-fluck-are-you look on her face.

Their eyes meet. He nods. Smiles. Intensely focused.

On her.

Damn. It happens. Even in his grateful reds, it happens.

She blurs around the edges. Girl parts strain to reach out and touch somebody.

And it sure isn't me.

Dr. Vic bustles in. No, a Dr. Vic clone. Her-not-her. Someone wound up, skin pulled too tight across the face. A brittle voice hers-not-hers launches into a recitation of the latest round of tests on Bishop.

Result: negative. But the antibiotics aren't completely effective.

This brittle delivery is so not Dr. Vic. Osmosis delivers her stress level to Bishop, who ticks wildly. Jerome is awed/cowered into silence. I think: for God's sake, pull the curtain shut around one of their beds.

Something Dr. Vic always, always does.

Curtains remain undrawn as med terms shoot from her mouth like machine-gun rounds. Dr. Vic repeats herself, stumbles, checks Bishop's chart again.

Silence at last. Save for the cloth-on-cloth of Bishop ticking.

"Dr. Seng, all them medical words turn into mumbo-jumbo on me," Bishop's mom finally says. "What was that last thing? Limp-something system?"

Dr. Vic turns to Tristan and says, "Would you explain the lymphatic system to Mrs. Wilson please, Tia?"

Molecules go critical, and the room swells with Dr. Vic's pain.

"Tristan," Dr. Vic whispers in apology. "I meant *Tristan.*"

I ache for her. I know that pain. But if there is something I should do for her, I don't know what it is. I know for sure there was nothing anyone could do for me. Time passes. You move. But the gaping hole remains.

Someone squeezes my hand quickly, then releases it.

So. He feels it, too.

Then he reels off textbook definition of the lymphatic system. Advanced textbook. Absolutely endless.

I think: Tristan, you utterly insensitive Brickhead Razzle-dazzler. Don't you see that Bishop's mom is clueless?

Then. Light dawns. He's buying time for Dr. Vic.

Dr. Vic pulls the curtains around Bishop's bed, and we all ease inside.

So. The insensitive Brickhead is me. Femme version.

"Okay, what you're telling me is you don't know what's wrong with my kid," Bishop's mom says. "You've tested him for every kinda illness, and my kid don't have none of 'em."

Dr. Vic rallies. "We've been very thorough. I'd like to repeat some of the tests, on the offchance that we got a false negative, however—"

"Dr. Vic, could I speak with you a minute?"

Wilma Urser, a.k.a. Red-Hot-Med-Student-Most-Likely - to -Moonlight - as - Jaws - Shark - Mother - Superior-at-Our-Lady-of-the-Humor-Free, sticks her cavernous mouth inside Bishop's curtained area.

"As you can see, I'm busy right now, *Ms.* Urser," Dr. Vic replies frostily. "See me later in my—"

"I'm afraid this can't wait," Jaws asserts.

Dr. Vic excuses herself. Tristan and I follow her into the hall. Possibly to protect her from Jaws.

"Interrupting me when I'm with a patient and a parent is unforgivable, Ms. Urser. See me in my office tomorrow morning—"

"Tomorrow is Sunday," Jaws points out.

"Fine, then, Monday. And you had better have an excellent explanation for this outrageous behavior—"

"You didn't test Bishop for HIV," Jaws interrupts.

Dr. Vic's jaw works.

Finally: "I'm sure I did."

"No, you didn't. And if I might speak frankly, for understandable reasons, you haven't been quite one hundred percent lately, Dr. Seng. So for the good of the patient, I brought this to Dr. Davis's attention."

Whoa. Unwritten rule at every hospital in the history of the universe: no lowly med student ever, *ever* goes over head of Doctor One to Doctor Two.

Addendum to unwritten rule: Especially not to rat out Dr. Vic.

Addendum to addendum: Especially not to rat out Dr. Vic to that Nazi-in-disguise Davis.

Jaws on a roll now, full steam ahead. "Dr. Davis ordered the AIDS test yesterday. It's been notated on Bishop's chart."

Dr. Vic pounded into the corner but manages to fight her way out. Shoulders go back. Chin up. "That you did what you thought best for the patient is laudable, *Ms.* Urser. However, the manner in which you did it makes me tremble for anyone, patient or colleague, involved in your future medical career."

The bell sounds—Dr. Vic gets paged—and that's the end of the round.

• • •

The endless morning ends, I head for Rick's room to meet Becky. His door is open. The bed's cranked. He and Becky both on it, holding hands. In plain sight.

"You must have a death wish," I say.

"That's what everyone tells me," Rick jokes. His voice is weaker, body frailer.

"I don't mean you."

Becky holds tight. "It's called therapeutic touch."

"But The Virus—" I protest.

She holds up their joined hands. "It's not like my head is bobbing under the sheets."

"Now, that's my idea of therapeutic touch," Rick says, but his eyes go half-mast. "Man, that shot they gave me is kickin' in. Sorry if I'm a crappy host."

Becky gets up, kisses his forehead, whispers something in his ear. I call a soft good-bye, but he's already out.

In the hallway she says, "Just don't say anything right now. Please."

Okay.

We're halfway home to the unsweet suite before she speaks again. "He's getting weaker."

Can't be denied. I nod.

"I had to stand there this morning while Dr. Coolidge examined Rick. Listened to his heart and his lungs. Coolidge let me listen, too. Then, outside, Coolidge says he estimates Rick's survival time absent a suitable heart-lung donor to be approximately six weeks."

Schlitz.

"Then he describes to me in excruciating detail exactly how and why, without a heart-lung transplant, this patient would expire. And just so you'll be ready, he expects you to take notes as he expounds," Becky goes on. "So I scribble down how horrible Rick's death is going to be in my notebook, like a good little student."

"God, Becky." I don't know what else to say. A donor will show up? Don't give up hope? Look for the silver lining? It's gonna be okay?

Please. The platitude posse has left the building.

We round the corner to the dorm. "Coolidge examined Shane this morning, too," Becky says, voice hard. Un-Becky. "He's doing great."

I know.

"I really friggin' hate him for that."

I know that, too.

What to say? I flip though mental file cards for something to distract close-to-tied-with-Erin-for-number-one-girlfriend from bottomless emotional crevasse.

Gossip.

Gossip is good. Always works with Erin.

Here's some: me, looking for The Secret Room. Open wrong door. Dr. B and Summer. As Jerome would say, entwined by design for a get-down time.

Now, *that's* gossip.

But. Same night as Rick and Shane's infamous coin flip. For sure that's not going to distract her. For sure I'm too chicken to bring it up.

I go for weak beans second best. Relay discovery of Summer's knockoff el cheap-o version of expensive De Rien perfume in trash, real-bottle-magically-full episode.

Distraction success.

"No schlitz?" Becky asks.

No schlitz.

"So what's up with that, do you think? Because I smell rich bitch on her like white on rice."

Me, with a shrug: "Maybe she's a *cheap* rich bitch."

Becky laughs singular full-bodied Becky laugh. I launch into distraction story number two. Eve. And Chad Q's morph into walking clipboard.

Bingo. Becky holds her stomach, howling with laughter, as we ascend to unsweet.

There, her skinny torso doing its best to hold up Tristan and Chad's door, blowing smoke rings, is NicoDaisy.

Or possibly NicoDots.

No. Tacky cheek-peek cutoffs give identity away. Definitely NicoDaisy. Tisha.

My guess: manhunt.

"Hey, 'zup?" she calls as we approach.

"Not much," Becky answers. "Can we help you?"

"Oh, no." She ciggie sucks. "Hey, this is where Tristan lives, right?"

Manhunt confirmation.

Her head bobs. "Cool." She flicks ashes, which rain on the floor.

"Would you mind not filling our hallway with your fallout?" Becky asks, sugar over spice.

"Oh, wow, sorry." Flustered, NicoDaisy flails around on patrol for nonexistent ash receptacle. Skull-and-crossbones motif fanny pack opens. Contents clatter to ashen floor.

We help her gather worldly goods—topless lipstick tube, cigs, Bic, wallet, keys. I reach for folded things behind me. Four hot-pink-and-silver foil-packed condoms.

Ladies' Choice.

I hand her Ladies' Choices. Mindlessly note nico-stained fingertips on little girl hands, which might later on hold Tristan.

Would he? Most guys would. Variety being spice, et cetera, et cetera.

But Tristan?

"So, you guys coming to the Bomb tonight?" NicoDaisy asks.

"Probably," I say.

"Cool. It's, like, a total blowout, you know? People get crazy, it's unreal." More ciggie suckage. "So, is Tristan gonna be there?"

Becky shrugs. "Ask him."

"Yeah, well, that's what I was planning on, only, like I been here for an hour, and the dude hasn't shown."

Golden male beauty appears at top of stairs.

"Lucky you," I say. "He just did."

She asks.

Tristan's reply: "Maybe."

Behind badly feigned cool, her face lights up. NicoDaisy has seized glimmer of hope offered by Object of Desire.

I think: This is how it is. One always the desire-er, the other the desired. Desired wields power of "maybe" over desire-er, able to offer hope without comfort. It's a thing with feathers. That it can so easily fly away is what makes it so tantalizing.

The caress of "maybe" is an ache.

Mine, not hers.

I flucking hate him for the power of "maybe."

Tisha launches a windy story about how she finally got her car out of the shop that day. Tristan listens. I unlock unsweet and push in.

The ceiling is ablaze with helium balloons. Dozens and dozens and dozens. Strings hang down like flipped exclamation marks.

"Festive," Tristan notes wryly, looking inside.

"Wow!" NicoDaisy breathes, longing for her room to be filled with Tristan's balloons. "Is it someone's birthday?"

"Not that I know of," Becky says, pulling at a string. There's a note taped to each balloon right below the tie. She pulls one down.

" 'You make me feel high,' " she reads.

" 'I'm ballooney tunes for you,' " I read from another.

Becky's face goes shiny. I'm thinking what she's thinking.

"From Rick," I pronounce, happy for her happiness, wondering how Rick got Summer to do this.

Becky is lit from within. "It's just so Rick, isn't it?"

I grab a string. " 'You tug the string to my heart,' " I read dramatically.

Buoyant as the bobbing globes, she grabs another.

Reads silently.

Her face goes slack.

"What's wrong?" Tristan asks.

Wordless, Becky hands him the balloon.

Tristan reads the note aloud. " 'I'm on the ceiling over seeing you tonight, Zoey. Greg.' "

10

ZOEY

"I'm telling ya, Zoey, he's into you," Becky insists for tenth time.

It's Erin redux. In response to my "Tristan is not into me."

They're both wrong.

Time: hours later. Place: unsweet. Sound track: *Rent,* from Becky's CD player. Action: dressing for the Bomb.

Correction. Becky dresses. I sit cross-legged on lumpy excuse for bed as dressed as I plan to get. Meaning comfy and baggy. No flesh flash. Prepared for hot date with Zen G. Read: use of non-lust-inducing nice guy in pitiful (as opposed to pathetic, pathetic comes later) attempt to make actual lust-inducing irritating guy jealous.

Raging maturity.

"What happened to his face when he realized all these balloons are for you from another guy?" Becky leans over, lifts glorious *I Know What Your Breasts Did Last Summer* into cups of strapless lacy demi-bra.

"It fell," I note.

"Aha," Becky retorts.

"As in, 'I feel badly for my friend Becky because she thought they were from Rick.' "

"No. As in, 'I'm jealous,' you idiot." Sheer white off-the-shoulder peasant blouse drops over her head.

Deadpan, I go, "I'm convinced. He's crazed for me, he's gonna admit it at the Bomb tonight, and then he's gonna kick that dog Summer to the curb."

Rent group lament ends. A moment of silence before next tune.

I hear deadpan, "Woof-woof."

Summer stands just inside the door. Her entrance evidently muffled by Broadway rock belters.

Ability to speak eludes me.

"Hi, Summer," says Becky, so caj, pulling up drawstring pants to just below navel. "Long time no see."

Summer drops Hermes bag on perfectly made bed. Read: Unslept-in bed because she was with *him*. Selects clothes from closet, lingerie wisps emerge from sachet-scented drawers. Wordless, into the bathroom. The door locks audibly behind her.

"Great, well, I'm glad we had this little chat," I

mutter. Hands—mine—cover my face as humilia-
tion—mine—reigns.

My bed sinks from Becky's weight. "Big effing
deal," she tells me, voice earnest. "It's not like she
didn't already know how you feel."

Sounds of a shower start.

"How do you know she already knew? God, this
is so high school."

"Your problem is, you let her psych you out."

"I do not—"

"She's a master mind-flucker," Becky insists.
"Look, in my neighborhood in New York, the His-
panic sistuhs don't take that kinda *drek* off anyone,
because—"

"Drek?"

"Schlitz, in Yiddish. It's all about 'tude. There's
this acting exercise my parents do, called Acting As
If. Say you want to convey a certain emotion, but
you don't feel it. You Act As If you do. Totally."

She checks out my reaction. Off my dubious look,
she adds, "If you act it totally, totally enough, it
becomes true. Get it?"

"She who mind-flucks first mind-flucks best?"

Becky nods. "Fastest mouth in the house."

I take this in. Mentally try it on. Zoey with 'tude.
Hot Okie momma. Get down with my bad self.

Can you spell *pathetic*? "It's so . . . not me."

Summer and smoke—read: very hot steam—
emerge from the bathroom. Low-key designer wear,
wet hair, makeup-free glowing skin.

Huh. Her normal toilette takes at least an hour.

Silently she plucks various items from drawers, throws them into straw bag, retrieves Hermes, heads for the door.

And then turns back to us.

Natch. Gotta go for the exit line.

"By the by, this bitch—as in female dog—won't be at the little beach party tonight," she drawls.

We take this in, say nothing.

Summer smiles. "I'd give a lot for a video of that trailer trash townie and you, the Okie jock who lacks what it takes to become a doc, both throwin' themselves at Tristy tonight. He and I could watch it together. Humor is great for foreplay. And I'm sure your video'd be way more entertainin' than any Blockbusters rental."

And she's gone.

Even Becky's momentarily nonplused. "She's good," she finally admits.

"Queen of the Triple Bs," I agree morosely.

"I wonder why she's not going to the Bomb."

"Dr. B."

Becky's looking at me like "huh?"

So I tell her what I saw.

I just don't tell her what night I saw it.

"She's doing Dr. Bailey?"

"Technically, I don't know. I wasn't present for actual . . . liftoff."

Becky jumps up, paces the room. "This is really bad, Zee. Very, very bad."

"Yeah, as in he's very, very married."

She whirls to me. "Don't you get it? Radio stations give away money, it's called dialing for dollars. How much can a girl make when she's doing it for dollars? *With the chief medical officer of the effing hospital?*"

Twenty-five thousand. My density is beyond. That she's doing Dr. B to guarantee herself the SCRUBS scholarship money never dawned.

Well. The sun sure as hell just came up. Because she is *not* going to fluck her way to that scholarship. That scholarship is mine.

Becky's still pacing. "You're sure neither of them saw you?"

"Sure."

"Okay. Threatening to expose her little doo-wop-diddy is out," Becky decides. "She'll deny it, Dr. B'll back her up, we look like vindictive lying bitches out to get her, and the whole thing blows up in our faces."

I'm sure your video'd be way more entertainin' than any Blockbusters rental.

"We video 'em." I'm kidding. But not.

"Yeah," Becky scoffs. "Uh, listen, Dr. B, could you just hold your left hand—yeah, the one with the wedding ring—right by Summer's nipple while I change the film?"

"C'mon, I was joking." Not. "We could tell his wife. Anonymously."

Our eyes meet. Mutually unspoken: too awful to hurt her to help us. Even if it is her hub's doing.

And then, brilliance strikes.

"I got it. We find out when and where and how

Summer's going down for the gold. Not tonight, but sometime soon. The Virus gets a note from someone—not us—telling her to be there for some vital reason. And then—"

"—she catches them, and I'm catching on." Becky's voice oozes admiration. "The Virus is desperate for Bailey's job. She'll nail both of their coffins shut while they're still breathing."

Our eyes meet again.

"You massively underestimate yourself, Zee. Your queen bitch po' is mind-blowing."

Yeah?

Funny. I feel lots of things.

But none of them are good.

Zen G and I are dancing.

"Told you it'd be wild!" he yells over vintage outlaw rock blaring from oversize speakers in flat-back of Fat Adam Sandler lookalike's truck, backed onto beach.

I nod. Know from former life in Okies not to compete with Lynyrd Skynyrd.

The Bomb bonfire is massive. Maybe a hundred people, maybe more, townies and Effing Huh's alike, party in its primal glow. A long table sags beneath food. Two steel kegs piss brew. Two wood barrels labeled GIVE TILL IT HURTS 'CUZ BREAST CANCER HURTS MORE are sunken in the sand. Everyone's dropped bills and coinage into the barrels.

Tristan's out there, somewhere, in the firelight.

I can't help thinking: without Summer.

I can't help thinking: while I'm with Zen G.

Zen G is: beyond nice. Kind. Sweet. Deeply into me.

Tristan is: none of the above.

Query to self: Act As If I'm into Zen G and make it so? Stop pursuit of unobtainable irritating object of mass female lust who lusts not for me? Abandon all hope, ye who enter here, but do it with a smile?

Shut up and dance.

Music goes slow. Bluesy. I step into Zen G's arms.

He murmurs into my hair.

"I want to thank you again for the balloons."

"I was afraid you'd think it was corny."

"No, it was sweet. Really. Just don't pick the lock again."

"Promise." He smiles. "I'll leave four, five dozen roses outside the door instead."

"You don't have to bring me—"

"We gotta do something about that lock of yours. Any butthole can slip a credit card in there, fiddle it around, and boom, he's in. I'm gonna worry about you."

" 'Sokay."

"No, listen, I'm putting a decent lock on tomorrow."

We sway to the music. A laughing couple, she clad only in bikini bottom, runs by us, splashing, shrieking into the ocean.

"D'you always wanna be a doctor?" Zen G asks.

"Yeah."

"Me, too," he says.

Him, too? Townie Zen G? EMT on a revved Harley?

Since when?

It occurs that I know next to nothing about him. Consumed with self-and-or-daily-*him* obsession and-or mental pity party, I've never asked. Cared to ask.

"This is dumb but . . ." I pull my head back so I can look at him. "I don't even know how old you are."

"The truth? Twenty-six."

Twenty-six? I thought twenty-one, maybe, but—

"Funny. Thought I'd be outta the Harbor a long time ago. And here I am."

"How come?"

He doesn't answer.

"Sorry, it's none of my—"

"It's not that," he says. Hesitates again, like he's trying to figure out what to say. "One time I was at this kick-ass Travis Tritt concert. I'm in the john, and this guy I never saw before starts tellin' me these intimate details of his life. I'm thinking, 'you poor, lonely schmuck. No matter what your deal is, your life is more sacred than to spill it to someone who doesn't know you while you're takin' a leak.' "

The weird thing is, I know exactly what he means.

He pulls me closer. It's not icky.

His husky voice in my ear. "You feel so good."

"So do you."

Did that just pop out of my mouth? It did. Acting As If? Or did I mean it?

Quickly survey level of fire down below. Girl parts are on perc. Many degrees from boiling over. But still.

"So, are Buddhists allowed to lust?" I ask.

He grins. "Hey, I figure we're all seeking Nirvana one way or another."

Something between us, against me, vibrates. Literally.

He reaches for his beeper, reads it. "Damn. I gotta call in. Don't suppose you've got a cell?"

I shake my head no.

"Be back soon." He kisses my forehead, sprints off.

Chad wanders over, eating scorched marshmallows off a stick. "Lose your date?"

"He got beeped. Eve here?"

"Real funny, little momma," he drawls, instant Elvis. "If she was here, I'd be buried in the sand by now. Head included."

He offers up scorcher 'mallow. I pop sticky mass in my mouth, suck it from my fingers. "She's really nice, Chad. *Nice* is a stupid, lame word. But . . . she really is."

"Zoey, she's everything."

"And what are you? Mold?"

"She's twenty-four, gorgeous, brilliant, accomplished, with this entire adult life. And I'm—I'm this barely eighteen-year-old kid. What do I have to offer her? Zero."

"Do or Dare!" a girl yells into cupped hands from the flatbed of Fat Adam's truck. "It's for charity, you cheap S.O.B.s, so get your butts over here."

Do or Dare? We're curious. We wander over. A crowd forms as the girl keeps up her harangue.

Sudden heat.

I know he's there before I look.

"Hey," says Tristan. "Having fun?"

"Sure." I watch firelight dancing in his eyes.

He nods. "Where's Greg?"

I don't say, "Got beeped, went to call in, be right back."

Instead I say, vaguely, "Around."

Because it makes me seem less with Zen G, more available.

Because basically, I suck.

"Your dates often lose interest in you this fast?"

So irritating. "He happens to be very interested," I insist. "He—"

From down the beach, a female screech, juvie version: "Tristan! This is so cool, you came! I've been looking for you everywhere!"

The call of the wild NicoDaisy. Obviously inebriated. New cheek-peeks in patriotic red, white, and blue. Color-coordinated tube top red with white stars.

NicoDaisy catapults self across sand. Takes flying leap at Tristan. Who can a) catch her. Or b) let her drop like sack of schlitz.

A. Her warm arms wrap around his neck, legs around his waist.

Yee-haw. Ride 'em, cowboy.

"I'm putting you down now," says Tristan.

She sticks out her lower lip, baby pouting. Wiggles against him to emphasis nonbaby point.

Chad watches in fascination. Me, too.

Mine, though, is masochistic.

"Now," Tristan repeats.

" 'Kay." She releases death grip on neck but locks legs around him. Drops backward. Hangs off his waist, upside down. "Givin' you ideas? Wow, I'm feelin' kinda . . ."

He eases her to the sand. Crouches down. "You okay?"

"Yeah. I just got dizzy there for a sec. Wow. So can you sit with me for a minute? Till I feel better?" She grabs his hand. He sits.

Puh-leeze.

Becky walks over eating a hot dog. Takes in Tristan and Tisha holding hands in the sand.

On Becky's amazement, "Don't even ask" is my comment.

"Zoey?" It's Zen G, looking mighty unhappy. "I used Larry's cell. Two EMTs on the graveyard shift got food poisoning at the Crab House. I gotta cover."

"Leave, you mean?"

He nods. "Damn."

Impulse to publically demonstrate affection for Zen G for benefit of hand-holding jerk on sand overwhelms. Impulse resisted.

Mature Zoey: "That's too bad. Some other time." A light kiss on the lips.

"I'll call you. And I'm changing that lock." His hand cups my cheek. Tenderly. Then he's gone.

Immature Zoey sneaks peek at hand-holding jerk on sand.

Who is not even looking in my direction.

Sometimes I *detest* him.

"All righty, studs and stud-ettes," calls the girl on the truck. "I'm Sharon, the best nurse in geriatrics, if I do say so myself—"

Much razzing in response.

"Do or Dare time. Guess your partner's 'do' wrong, it's ten big ones in the charity barrel. Refuse the dare, same thing. Who's our first brave duo to step up to the truck?"

Laughter, pushing, jostling. Fat Adam climbs into flatbed to applause and whistles. Lifts laughing spike-haired woman with tasteful multiple piercings.

"Is this like Truth or Dare?" Becky asks. I shrug. So does Chad. Everyone seems to know what's going on but us.

"Go for it," says Sharon.

Fat Adam scratches his chin. "Here it is. Lori, who'd you do, Bob Dole or Elizabeth Dole?"

Raucous ewws from the crowd.

"Join a convent!" someones yells.

"Neither, man!" Lori goes, laughing.

"Gotta do one, them's the rules," Sharon says. "What's Lori gonna say?" She leans over to Fat Adam, who whispers in her ear.

Lori squeezes her eyes tight, scrunches up her face, yells, "I gotta do . . . Elizabeth!"

"Yes!" Fat Adam's fist pumps the air. "Do I know

my woman?" He hoists her over his shoulder, smacks her butt, and carries her off.

Just another touching example of Neanderthal love.

"Hey, you two, drop some bucks in the bucket, anyway," Sharon instructs them. "Who's next? Up and at 'em!"

Leo helps Allie, clad in usual dottie bikini—into flatbed. Her eyes scan the beach. "Tish?"

Miraculously cured, Tisha abandons future husband, a.k.a. Tristan, moves through crowd to chants of "Tish-a! Tish-a! Tish-a!"

She climbs into flatbed, offers up tube-topped shimmy. Allie fist-bumps her. Someone hands Tisha a lit cigarette. Do they know their bud or what?

"Okay, girls, who's up?"

"I'll ask," Allie decides. "Who would you do, Tisha, our English teacher, Mr. Gabanski, or . . . Tori Spelling?"

Hilarity ensues. Allie whispers guess in Sharon's ear.

Tisha bites lower lip. "I'd do . . . Gabanski!"

"Wrong!" Sharon cries. "Ten big ones in the barrel. What's her dare, Allie?"

"Mmmmm . . . let's see. Tisha has to demonstrate how she'd . . . kiss Gabanski with . . . Tristan!"

He rises. Slow and easy, heads for the flatbed. Flips himself into it.

"A peck won't do for Do or Dare," Sharon points out.

Tristan, that brasspole, smiles.

Tisha goes for it. Tongue bathes male intestinal organs. Horny dogs and firepoles come to mind.

The crowd goes wild.

Mental song begins.

> *This is the kiss that never en-n-nds,*
> *It just goes on and on my frie-e-e-ed ...*

Huh. Look at that. If alcoholic waitress career path doesn't work out for NicoDaisy, porn star has possibilities.

"It's just a stupid game," Becky murmurs.

Endless kiss actually ends. The crowd cheers. Tisha bows, takes deep drag off ciggie. Ready to sign autographs with Tristan's boy parts.

Which works better if you wet the tip first.

Someone throws bottle of Jack at flatbed. Tristan makes a one-handed grab. Tisha takes it. Bottoms-up.

"Chug-chug-chug!" chant ensues.

"This is so not fun anymore," Becky decides.

Tristan tries to pry bottle from Tisha. Who falls into his arms. Studly surfboy carries her out of flatbed.

Oh, Scarlett. Oh, Rhett.

Frankly, I don't give a damn.

"Let's get out of here," I say.

"You guys up for Aesop's?" Becky asks.

Chad nods. "Lemme get Tristan and we can—"

"He's occupied," I snap.

"Come on, what was he supposed to do, dis the

chick in front of everyone, and not go up there?"

"Now, there's an option," Becky says.

Chad shakes his head. "That's cold. I'm gonna go tell him we're leaving, he can do whatever he wants. I'll meet you on the boardwalk."

Fifteen minutes later Chad, Becky, and I sip Icy Fiends at an Aesop's outdoor table. Smells Like Tuna wails the blues inside.

Chad and Becky go in to dance. My dancing mood has boogied off for the night. I sit alone.

Pity party commences anew. All around me the look of love. It's everywhere. I wan'cha and right back a'cha.

What have they got that I haven't got? What pathetic psycho defect makes me want him so much? When he wants me even less than flucking Nico-Daisy?

The truth: Tonight, no Summer. And Tristan still didn't want me.

I must be wishing on someone else's star.

So. Acting As If I'm over him begins. As of now.

Into steamy Aesop's den of sin I go. Grab first guy I see. Dance myself sweaty. Go guy to guy. Flirting, dancing. Check in with Chad and Becky now and then. Go back for more. It's easy, really.

Mindless fun. Kinda. Kinda not.

Until after who knows how long, he has the nerve. To show up. And ruin. Everything.

I'm leaning against the wall fanning myself. "Go away."

"I could have sworn I was invited to this party."

"I just uninvited you."

"Why?"

Amazing. Tristan actually looks like he doesn't know.

"Shocking pink Ladies' Choice ring any chimes?"

He's not telling. Imagine. Studly *and* gallant.

I say, "You and Summer really deserve each other, you know that?"

"Would you mind telling me what you're so pissed off about?"

Deep breath. Calm Zoey. "It's like this, Tristan. Tisha is a not very bright girl with a not very bright future, a not very manageable alcohol problem, and a not very mature crush on you. For you to use that is so disgusting that—"

His eyes go granite.

"You think I had sex with her?"

"Let me put it this way. I think you joined in that little porn performance, got a little overheated, Summer wasn't around so, what the hell, you carried Tisha off for a quick anatomy lesson."

His eyes fix on mine.

"Look, it doesn't matter what I think," I go on. "It has nothing to do with me." I look around. "Where's that hot guy I was just dancing with?"

Tristan grabs my arm.

Hard.

"Let go of me."

He does. "I'm sorry. That was—I'm sorry."

My arm doesn't hurt. I Act As If and rub it anyway. "Just when I thought you never got mad. But then maybe you loosen up after The Ice Man Cometh."

He's silent. Then, finally. "Funny thing, Zee. How much you detest people who put people into little boxes. And how good you are at it."

Stung.

"Is that supposed to put me on defense?" I ask.

He's unmoved. "You know nothing about Tisha. And if you think I did anything more than be kind to her, make sure she was okay, and make sure Allie was going to be driving Tisha home tonight instead of the other way around, you know nothing about me, either."

He turns. Walks away.

I can't move. His words nailed me.

Every part of me, even parts I didn't know I had, tell me: he spoke nothing but the truth.

Schlitz.

I run. After him. "Tristan—"

He's out the door, heading for Effing-Huh.

"Tristan, I'm sorry. *Don't go.*"

Torn from my throat. A terrible loss. Almost like that nightmare loss. That's crazy.

But it's what I feel.

"Tristan—"

Suddenly he stops. Turns to me. And I'm in his arms. His lips are on mine. Bruising me. Oh, God. Oh, God. I want him. Want him to. Want him to—

Dimly heard, brakes screech. The sound is piercing but not to me, lost in Tristan.

"Watch out!"

"Oh, my God!"

Shattering screams. We break apart.

11

TRISTAN

The car veers off the street and careens through the outdoor tables of Aesop's like a bowling ball, mowing down everything in its path—tables, chairs, people.

It's heading right for us.

With all my might I push Zoey away, then dive. Tires roll just past my right foot. Then I'm up again, but helpless, as it crashes through the big glass front window and finally comes to a smoking rest with an ominous thud.

Surreal. Glass everywhere, shattered tables and chairs, people moaning, screaming, crying for help.

And blood. So much blood. In the distance, sirens.

Dazed people climb out through the shattered window. One girl holds her arm, gushing blood. Arterial, has to be, to make a fountain like that. She looks at it curiously, not sure it belongs to her.

Then she collapses.

I'm on it, ripping off my shirt to make a tourniquet, wrapping it tightly around her arm.

Becky's cheek bleeds a little as she holds a tablecloth against some guy's head wound.

The girl whose arm I'm holding opens her eyes, looks up at me like a jacked deer.

"You're okay," I assure her quietly. "Lie still."

"Get away from the car!" Chad yells over the hellish din. "Everyone, get away from the car. It could explode, move it!"

People scatter. But Chad moves toward the car. To see who's inside. To try and help them.

The person I don't see is Zoey. Where did she land, after I pushed her? If anything happened to her . . .

You can't petition the Lord with prayer, a seminary teacher—not mine—once said. I know that's true, too. Experience has taught me that much.

So screw that. I act.

I have to find Zoey. If she's near the car, under it, hurt, bleeding, can't get away, and the car explodes . . .

I'm calling for someone to come hold the tourniquet on this girl's arm so I can go to the car, when—

Whoosh!

The car's engine ignites in a burst. Dante's *Inferno*. Chad, half in the car, stumbles backward on fire. A big bearded guy tackles him, bats the flames out.

Where the hell is Zoey?

I get some guy to hold the tourniquet and fly toward the raging fire, holding my arm in front of my face. It's so damn hot. "Zoey? Zoey?" I'm screaming.

The fire station is only three blocks away. So the firefighters arrive with extinguishers on full throttle. They're at the car, trying to get the occupants out, but the front of the car bashed into a support pole, and the pole has smashed the engine into the passenger compartment.

Ambulances skid in. Paramedics and emergency personnel take over. They set up a field hospital to tend to the walking wounded and triage the rest.

I go to Chad. "You okay?"

He nods, sitting with his back against a wall. His face is black, hair singed, but his burns look minor.

"There are two people in that car," he says, his voice breaking. "Girls. They were alive, I saw 'em moving. But I couldn't get to them."

I squeeze his shoulder, because anything I say would be insulting.

Most important things are beyond words.

The fire is down to a smoldering, stinking mess, as more ambulances race up.

Where is flucking Zoey?

Greg jumps out of an ambulance, spots me, stops. "Is Zoey here?"

"Yeah." I don't add that I can't find her.

"Is she—"

"Greg, over here!" another paramedic yells to him from what's left of the car.

He peers inside. "Oh, Jesus," he mutters hoarsely. He reaches his hand into the car before a firefighter grabs him, as the Jaws of Life work to pry apart the twisted metal that used to be a car, to get at whatever is left of whoever was inside.

"We should go back to the ER, see if we can help," a voice at my side says.

Zoey.

Uninjured, it seems. Unless you count the ghosts that have taken over what used to be the pupils of her eyes.

I don't hug her or tell her how scared I was that she was hurt. Just nod my agreement. Chad and Becky agree, too.

Zoey half-smiles, or tries to. "You think maybe we're walking disaster magnets?"

Becky hugs her, hard. And then we're all jogging toward Effing-Huh.

FHUH ER is in action already when we get there. It's impressive. The Virus, Dr. Vic, Agonetti, and that sadistic son-of-a-bitch Davis are all on hand, as well as lots of others, some I've never seen before.

Some of the ambulances have arrived, others are on their way.

Davis is hurrying from one stretcher to another, stops when he sees us. "What the hell are you doing here?"

"We came to help, sir," Chad pipes up.

"The only way you can help is by getting the hell out of the way," he barks, "or I'll ream you a new—"

The last part is lost as he charges off.

But before we can decide what to do, Dr. Vic spies us and hurries over. Her eyes are too bright. She's hyperalert, in overdrive control. "SCRUBS, this is an excellent learning opportunity. Spread out, only one of you in each examining room. Mr. March, see what you can do for the friends and relatives waiting out there. Calm them down. It's so important to be calm during an emergency."

She's gone. For a moment, the four of us just stand there. We all know it, though nothing more has been said.

Something is deeply wrong with Dr. Vic.

Becky is the obvious choice for delegated comforter of utterly panicked friends and relatives awaiting word on their loved ones.

Chad, maybe. Zoey, even.

But me?

The only person less likely than me to calm the bereaved is Summer, and she's not here.

So, I'm passing out Dixie cups of water, offering putrid coffee from the machine, and my mind is on this established mathematical formula.

Saturday night between ten P.M. and three A.M. equals jammed hospital emergency rooms.

It's the demon C_2H_2OH. The active ingredient in beer. Wine. Tequila. (Just ask Billie. No, don't.

Don't talk about that again. Ever. What's the point? There is no do-over.)

I like a good buzz. Sometimes I like a bad buzz. What I don't like—hate, more like—are the scum folk who drink and drive. See, C_2H_2OH plus internal combustion engine plus wheels plus schmuck behind the wheel equals stupid-ass potential killer on the road. And way too often these scum folk fulfill that potential.

A couple of Saturday nights Ira literally flew me in to the hospital in Barrow to take in the ER follies. Method to my madness, he'd say. An opthalmologist like me doesn't rate a pulse with an adrenaline junkie like you, Tristan.

ER should be right up your alley.

Quite the show it was. Everything from broken-armed students who decided to play beer football to couples who drunkenly decided to demonstrate their mutual affection by bashing each other's heads with empty Bud bottles.

But that's northern Alaska. Down here, in so-called civilization, we get the real killers.

Drunk drivers. The oh, man, I was drunk, I didn't mean to hit a tree head on, kill my wife, run over a kid.

I give a hollow-eyed woman working rosary beads a Dixie of water, and think: it's a long way to Effing-Huh from the Arctic Circle.

The ER doors burst open as another ambulance arrives. Greg and some other guy run with the stretcher, calling into his walkie-talkie, "Trauma team, stat, Caucasian female, age 18, massive damage to central body due to compression by heavy object, third degree burns, internal bleeding, shock, BP 90 over 50 and falling, she's coding on us."

I follow him. The trauma team is there. They're unloading two bodies. The barely alive girl on Greg's stretcher, and the other girl from the car.

She's draped. Head under cotton.

Schlitz, as Zoey would say. Wholly sheeted.

Greg falls back against the wall as the trauma team takes over. "Kill me," he moans to no one.

I pull Greg outside, into fresh air. He moves on autopilot. "I killed her, I killed her, it's my fault."

"Who?" I ask him.

It's like he's talking to himself. "I was supposed to take care of her. I promised her brother, man. Promised. But I finally met a woman who is so sensational, who seems to be as into me as I'm into her, and then I got so pissed that they called me into work, and I just—I forgot. I didn't check on her. I just left. I left her, man. She got so toasted. Why didn't Allie drive? Why?"

I'm in a cold sweat. Sick. Filling in the blanks.

The sensational woman is Zoey.

Tisha and Allie were in that car.

But I made sure Allie had Tisha's keys. Allie promised me she'd drive Tisha's car. I believed her. Because I wanted to. Because I wanted to get to Aesop's.

To a sensational woman.

My mother the cynic always says, no good deed goes unpunished.

"Which one came in DOA?" I ask. But I already know. I saw the passenger side of the deathmobile.

"Allie," Greg confirms. Tears stream down his cheeks.

Dr. B's sleek brown Mercedes with the tinted windows pulls up. Clearly, the main man has been beeped. He jumps out and races past us. Everyone jokes about those can't-see-inside windows. Like, what does a straight-arrow guy like Dr. B need with tinted windows?

Suddenly Greg bolts, rushes through the swinging doors into the ER. I follow, but he's sacked by a couple of security guards as he's running into the trauma unit.

He breaks down in their arms. I mean, he just loses it, totally. Keeps crying that it's his fault.

I just stand there. Standing the stand of he who silently shares the blame.

A scent on the air. One I know well, react to viscerally.

De Rien.

I turn, and there's Summer in a soft white sundress. She walks toward me.

"Hey," she says softly. "What happened?"

I tell her. And I tell her who it happened to.

"Drunks make me sick," she says venomously. "God, those two stupid little girls. I'm going in to help," she adds briskly.

I watch her walk away. Achingly beautiful. And I think three things.

Thing one. Those "stupid little girls" are the same age she is. But Summer is no kid. Hasn't been for a long, long time. Just like me. But in her case, I don't know why.

Thing two. How intense her reaction was to drinking. Intensity born of something personal. But what?

Thing three. How did she know to come to the hospital?

I think about Dr. B's infamous tinted-windows Mercedes. Recall him getting out.

And I wonder: does the leather interior of that Mercedes smell of De Rien?

I'm up on the Effing-Huh roof solo four hours later, breathing.

My father told me a story once, about an Inupiat elder who had gotten very sick. No one could cure him. He kept telling them to take him outside, but it was multiple degrees below zero out, so of course no one listened.

To their amazement, when no one was looking, he crawled outside himself. Whereupon he shouted to the northern lights that two things had to be done under the sky.

Living.

And dying.

And then, he died. Peacefully, so it's said.

Me, I'm still living. Breathing. Trying for peaceful, but it's just so damn hard sometimes.

From behind me I hear the door. Dr. Vic steps out, silhouetted for a moment before the door shuts and blocks the indoor light again. I don't want to scare her. So I call softly to her from the dark.

"Hey, it's Tristan."

She's still, her eyes adjusting to the darkness. Then she walks over to me.

"Hi." Her voice is so weary. "I didn't think I'd find you here."

"My great escape," I tell her, and find my own voice is just as weary. Compare my pain to hers, though? Oh, hell. How do you gauge human suffering?

I have an overwhelming urge to hug her. I don't.

"What's the verdict downstairs?" I ask.

"It's under control, for now. Twelve injured. Mostly fairly minor—contusions, lacerations from glass, broken bones. One young man's in serious condition with a ruptured spleen. One young woman is critical—third degree burns, multiple fractures, internal bleeding. She's comatose, on a ventilator. I don't know if she'll make it through the night. She was driving the car. One young woman dead. The passenger. She asphyxiated."

I'm bewildered. "But the firefighters got there so fast. How did she—?"

"There was a case of foam cups on the backseat," Dr. Vic explains.

I understand instantly.

The biggest danger from many fires isn't from the flames, it's from the smoke. Styrofoam, when it burns or melts, produces acrilein, a chemical in the formaldehyde family. Formaldehyde is great for pickling fish. Or for preserving human parts during an autopsy.

But if you're alive, it's hell on your lungs.

So Chad was right. They both *had* been alive before the car caught fire.

If I could just go back to the Bomb. Ignore Allie when she promised me she'd drive, for sure. Stay and drive both of them myself, then none of this would—

No do-overs. I'm so sorry, Billie. All over again.

"The dead girl is Allie Drew," Dr. Vic goes on, her voice strangely flat. "The one in critical is Tisha Henry. I had to inform the parents. It's always horrible, but this was . . ." She doesn't finish that statement. Then adds, "I knew them both slightly. They're friends of Leo's."

"I know them, too."

Dr. Vic raises her eyebrows at me.

"Leo introduced us."

"Leo knows everyone," Dr. Vic says. "Except Leo."

No comment from me. None called for. It's not unusual for someone much older than me to treat me as an equal. I'm comfortable with that. But Dr. Vic is a doctor. And I am a lowly SCRUB. The Effing-Huh caste system puts India's to shame.

So why is she confiding in me?

We both look over the parapet wall toward the ocean. From far away, somewhere, out there, down there, someone laughs. Laughable but not funny.

"It never ends," she tells the unseen ocean. "I keep trying to do my best, but it feels like running in place. People die anyway. Tia. Allie. Then someone else, then someone else, then someone else."

"Maybe you need to take a break," I say, my voice low. "Your stress level has to be—you need time."

She laughs bitterly. "I ask for a leave, Pace'll bounce me off the fast track at this hospital so fast I'll be sewing up stitches at Main Street UrgentCare. Doctors deal with it. That's what we do. If you can't, then you don't belong here."

She's right.

"I knew a wonderful surgeon, brilliant man," she goes on. "He diagnosed himself with MS at the height of his career. Sometimes he was fine, other times—and he never knew when it would be—his left hand would go so weak that he couldn't use it. But he didn't tell anyone. How could he? His career would have been over. And besides, he knew he was a better surgeon with one hand than any other surgeon with two."

"But he owed it to his patients—"

"Yes. But he owed them his genius more. That's what he thought. Until a patient died who should have lived."

"What did he do?"

"He blew his brains out."

Silence.

"How could I have missed testing Bishop for HIV?" she asks me suddenly. "How could I do that?"

Her beeper goes off, and she looks at it. Her hand is shaking.

"Peds," she reports. "Test results."

She means Bishop. I know without her saying.

She returns her beeper, doesn't look at me. "I would appreciate it if you would . . . accompany me."

This brilliant, beautiful, kind, wounded woman. I would accompany her anywhere.

Silently we walk the flights to the peds floor together.

Peds is quiet. Just Lark Peyton and a floater at the nurses' station. A tiny TV-VCR combo is playing an episode of a soap opera which they both watch avidly. They must tape the soaps during the day to watch while on night duty.

"Ms. Peyton?" Dr. Vic asks. "The test results?"

Lark snatches up a manila envelope and hurries over. Doctors don't react joyfully to finding nurses engrossed in television while on duty. Lark barely looks at me as she hands Dr. Vic the folder.

"Thank you." Dr. Vic opens it. Reads. Her face registers zero. She hands the chart back to Lark. Then turns and wordlessly heads back to the door that leads to the stairs.

Back to the roof. This time I'm uninvited.

So I stand at the nurses' station while Lark shifts into heavy flirt mode. She's very good at it.

Something inside me goes on red alert. The un-invited decides to crash Dr. Vic's solitude.

I rush up the stairs to the roof. I open the door.

Dr. Vic is at the parapet wall. She hears me but doesn't turn around.

That tells me the results of Bishop's HIV test better than her words ever could.

The kid has Tourette's syndrome. Plus he's HIV positive.

And Dr. Vic is leaning over the parapet wall.

12
ZOEY

Online IRC chat
mario-ole!@wanadoo.su
zthemind@juno.com

Erin: Okay, I'm back. Mario was wiggin' cuz he couldn't find his effing cufflinks.

Zoey: Over missing links? Maybe he *is* the missing link. What's it have to do with you, anyway?

E: I kiss it and make it all better.

Z: Gag.

E: Not if you open wide and say "ah." I slay me.

Z: That makes one of us. You sure Mario isn't violent?

E: Can you just get over it? Please? So where were we?

Z: I just related horror story of car accident three days ago. Zen G is emotional wreck. Tisha's still alive. Barely. Allie's funeral is tomorrow.

E: Sucks. Speaking of which, 'zup with you and Surf Stud?

Z: Very Erinesque segue. You suck.

E: And swallow but only when it's true love. So?

Z: He kissed me.

E: !!!!

Z: Right before the car accident.

E: ????

Z: It was a pissed-off kiss, not an I'm-into-you kiss.

E: Ooo, hot angry kiss, I love those.

Z: Unkink thyself for a moment, please. He and I are now less than zero. Blames self for not driving Tisha and Allie home. Blames me, it feels like.

E: Ask him.

Z: Kinda tough. We're not speaking.

E: ????

Z: Who the fluck knows. He hasn't said two words to me since. I enter, he exits.

E: Enter backward. In a thong. You have a great ass.

Z: Gee, what a great idea, I'll send you a Xerox.

E: Sign it: To Mario, Lust & XXX

Z: Triple gag. When you gonna lose Triple M?

E: After he opens major Swiss bank acct in my name.

Z: Be sure to write conspic thank you note to Tri M's WIFE.

E: She doesn't speak Engli—Oh! I get it. You're taking correspondence course from the Skank.

Z: Unfunny.

E: Sanctimonious Butthole 101.

Z: Still unfunny. Triple M wigs me. You're sponging off him in foreign lands.

E: Sponges have nothing to do with it.

Z: Know the golden rule?

E: Duh.

Z: He who has the gold, rules.

E: Okie sister variation #1: She who gets his gold, drools?

Z: C'mon, E. This is so not you.

E: You're trippin and I'm playing. Wanna know where Triple M rates on Erin's Do The Nasty Hit Parade?

Z: No.

E: Liar. If Jason Lust Monster Marley from junior year was all-time high, and Rick Get Me My Viagra Barton from senior year was all-time low, Triple M is slightly below mid-pack, rising with a bullet. Plus he's buying me a Viper.

Z: ???

E: Badass car, you ignorant anti-slut. I'll be hottest thing in Tornado Alley. Worth kissing a little hairy

Z: Thank you!

E: Tomorrow we're . . . oops, his Triple M-ness bellows my name. Gotta go.

Z: You're at his every beck and bellow?

E: Crap, he sounds polluted, just a sec 'cuz

Z: Cuz what?

I wait for Erin to finish message. And wait. And wait. Zip.

Z: YO, ERIN! YOU THERE??

Re-wait. Zippage. Check time. Gotta get to Effing-Huh. *Où est la belle Okie?* Try to squash image of Triple M going off on her. Fail. Try to talk self into belief I'm overreacting due to blood-and-guts SurroundSound that is my *Groundhog Day.*

Failareeno.

Z: E-MAIL ME SOONER THAN ASAP—I'M WORRIED.

I log off puter. Can't log off foreboding. Grab backpack, keys, head out the door.

Just as *he* heads out of his.

This I know: A) relatives of Chad's are visiting Fable Harbor. He stayed at lux beach cottage with them for past two nights. B) Summer's bed unslept in for past two nights.

This I deduce: C) Tristan had someone whispering De Rien in unsweet across the hall the last two nights.

"Hey," he says now, dropping keys into his pocket.

"You look like Schlitz," I observe. Pure truth. He looks exhausted. A barely encroachment on usual perfection.

We head for the stairs.

I ooze sarcastic sympathy. "It really sucks when something as trivial as the opportunity to study medicine during the day interferes with your opportunities to study anatomy by night."

Awesome verbal surface lure designed to piss him off dangles in air. Damn fish doesn't rise to it.

I'm stinkbait. Repellent.

More walking.

'Kay. The kiss never happened. For sure he wishes it never had. Fine. Forgive and forget.

Only I can't. But never say—

I'm so sick of the wuss that is me.

So. New Zoey swings brass ones. We're halfway to Effing-Huh. I speak up. Correction. Squeak up.

"Are we ever going to . . . talk?"

He shrugs. "Words are overrated."

"Sorry. Guess my mind-meld skills aren't up to yours."

No reaction.

Itals mandatory: I will *not* let him run this show. Run me away. Make me insane. It's over—whatever *it* is—as of *now*.

We're about to enter the lobby. My hand is on his arm. He stops.

Me, on his regard of me: "Look, I know you're sorry you kissed me, okay? Between your double midnight peejay party with Summer and your treating me like bubonic plague, I kind of get the message. What I don't get is why—"

"Hey, you guys!" Cheerful Chad calls, jogging toward us. "My uncle took us out for this massive breakfast, s'why I'm late. We'd better move, huh?"

We stride toward the ER, where we're scheduled to meet with Dr. Vic. Running too late to don dreadful reds.

"Hey, where were you last night, man?" Chad asks Tristan. "I came by like at two—my relatives are serious party animals—I needed another change of clothes. Dumb me forgot my key, so I knocked and knocked."

"Musta been sound asleep," says Tristan.

Lie, lie, lie. Read: "Musta been demonstrating *Kama Sutra* love position #43 to Female Perfection. Didn't want to move the chandelier. Sorry."

At ER nursing desk Davis is reaming out Hirsute. Cause? Who knows? Becky and Summer stand near, in reds. Dr. Vic is nowhere in sight.

"You got that through your thick skull?" Davis asks Hirsute.

Hirsute sports double armpit ponds. "Sorry, Doctor," she whispers. "It won't happen again."

"It had better not."

Davis spots us, his disgust-ometer level goes to eleven.

"I plan to waste as little as possible of my valuable time on the five of you this morning," he barks, "so let's cut to the chase. Dr. Seng is—"

He stops, eyes Tristan. Me. Chad.

"Where are your reds?"

Chad and I lose ability to speak.

"We were running late, and usually for Dr. Seng's morning meeting she doesn't mind if—" Tristan says easily.

"Incorrect," Davis snaps. "Ask me why."

Tristan remains silent.

Davis jumps into Great Santini past life and gets in Tristan's face. Like *this* close.

"The answer is: there is no room in medicine for a little dipstick pretty boy like you who thinks he can get away with not wearing his uniform 'cause he's 'running late.' Do you see Ms. Silver and Ms. Everly not wearing their scrubs?"

Tristan's look: blank.

Davis waves medical records in the air. "See this, pretty boy? Fifteen-year-old third-world punk just got brought in by his friends. Why? Seems Flaco was hallucinating. Pupils dilated. All the symptoms of being raging drunk, right? Pretty boy like you waltzes in, running late, calls it alcohol overdose. Figures Flaco will sleep it off.

"But the doctor who is *on time, on top of it*, notices that the punk's face is frozen," Davis goes on. "Gets the punk's idiot friends to admit he'd eaten mushrooms his grandmother uses for decoration 'cause someone told him it would get him high. 'Shrooms looked like a shriveled brain, idiot friends report."

Davis moves even closer to Tristan. "So, Flaco ingested a *Gyromitra esculenta*. Deadly poisonous. Had to be lavaged immediately. Congrats, pretty boy who runs late. You woulda killed him."

The only sound: Davis's breaths of triumph. Then he turns and walks.

Tristan reels it off: "Vomiting, diarrhea, muscle cramps, acute abdominal pain, and seizures."

Davis stops, whirls, pumps. *"What?"*

"The symptoms of ingesting *Gyromitra esculenta*," Tristan says. "But Flaco is symptomatic for ingestion of an *Amanita muscaria*, more commonly known as fly agaric. It affects voluntary muscle movement. That's why his face is frozen."

Davis turns the color of a transfusion. "And just how the hell would you know that?"

"It's common in certain tropical climes to pulverize *Amanita muscaria* and mix it with sugar water. It's an inexpensive lure for houseflies. They sip it, become instantly paralyzed, drop and die. In Hawaii, we call it the assumpta."

Two beats.

Davis turns to Hirsute.

"Don't just stand there like a hairy warthog, get the Poisondex data on *Amanita muscaria* stat!"

Back to Tristan. "Your late arrival goes in your report, March. Yours, too," he adds to me and Chad.

Summer's French-manicured index finger flutters skyward.

"Ms. Everly?" Davis asks.

"Sir, you were about to tell us about Dr. Seng?"

"Yes. She's on a leave of absence until further notice. Your assignment today is do whatever the hell you want as long as you stay out of the way of the medical personnel who actually belong here."

Time to make our getaway. Becky cocks head toward door to nurses' lounge. We all head for it.

I drop into nearest chair. Becky pours swill from Mr. Coffee. "That man has a real problem," she comments. "And what's up with Dr. Vic?"

Shrugs everywhere.

"I knew she was wiggin', but—ugh." Becky sips swill, makes a face. "If I wasn't a scummy serf, I'd call her."

"But you are," Don Q Chad says, puffing air between his lips. "We can ask Leo. Unless he's lost it, too. Man. Another funeral."

Feels like we're already at one. Ours.

"Hey, I was up in peds this morning," sunny Becky says. "You know how Jerome's been begging them to move Bishop out? Well, I caught Jerome giving Bishop his Gameboy."

"To play with?" I manage.

"No, to keep," Becky said. "Weird, huh?"

"Did he tell you his homies would ice you if you ratted him out for being nice?" Chad asks, laughing.

Becky shakes her head. "Don't get too excited. As soon as Jerome sees, he goes, 'Yo, Becks, pretty momma, nice *green* shirt.' "

I lose it in laughter. Everyone else, too.

Even Summer.

"I can't figure out how a kid that age could turn HIV positive," Becky goes on. "The blood supply was cleaned up way before he was born, so he couldn't have gotten it like that. Obviously it wasn't through sexual contact—"

"His father is an ex-junkie with full-blown AIDS," Summer says stonily.

Huh? I read Bishop's chart. That isn't there.

How does she know?

She isn't saying.

"People don't get AIDS by living with a family member who has it," Chad points out.

"Bishop doesn't live with him," Summer says. "Pop's out of the picture."

"How do you know so much about this?" Don Q asks.

"I study, Chad," says Summer sweetly. "And I listen. But only to the right people. A skill you might cultivate if you plan to ever get ranked higher than last in our little group."

Becky to Summer: "I know you get off on being a bitch. What I don't know is why."

Summer smiles. "Because I'm so good at it."

I check out Tristan.

This is the girl you want? This?

He's unreadable. Mentally elsewhere.

Fluck. It's way too much. Tia, Allie, Tisha, Dr. Vic. Erin with Quad M (read: add Mentally unbalanced) Mario. My mind reels, my head lolls. "Someone say something good, 'cuz I'm O.D.ing on bad."

Becky to the rescue. "Rick's hanging in there. Even Dr. Cool said so."

"That *is* good."

Chad squeezes her shoulders. "He's gonna make it, Becky. God won't let Rick die. I really believe that."

My BP soars.

What, Chad? God decided to make sure there was no traffic jam on the interstate so that everyone could get to work on time but so that parents would get to OKC just in time to die, but God won't let Rick die? How does that work, Chad? In what messed-up mindset? In what messed-up universe?

They keep talking Schlitz. BP 180 over 95. I close eyes: Munch's most famous painting appears. I'm ready to, too. BP 185 over 1—

Summer's voice: "How'd you know all that material on poison mushrooms?"

"Read it," Tristan says.

Am distracted enough to open eyes.

"Very impressive, Mr. March," Summer drawls. Sounds like commentary on his perfing of acts still illegal in some states. "Missed you last night. Night before, too."

Tristan mutters something unintelligible.

I hear her reply. "Tonight, then. See all of you then."

My eyes open. She's out the door.

An insipid story problem from sixth grade math comes to mind:

If Summer did not sleep at home for two nights, and Summer was not with her boytoy Tristan those nights, where did Summer sleep if Dr. B was home with Dr. B's wifey as could commonly be assumed to be true? And if when Chad knocked on Tristan's door after midnight and Tristan wasn't home but Tristan wasn't in the dunes with Summer nor at Dr. B's home with Dr. B's wifey, where was Tristan?

Always got A's in math.

But this quiz, I flunk.

"Good news, Tisha's off her ventilator," reports Nancy Galespie a.k.a. N.G. a.k.a. Engie, Effing-Huh's number-one kick-ass ICU burn unit nurse. Engie's short, squat, big-nosed.

More beautiful than I will ever be.

"She still comatose?"

"Semi. Her vitals look better. I think she's gonna make it."

Tisha is in special bed for burn victims, semifloating. She is peeled like rotting fruit, to make new skin. Bandages cover all but eyes, fingertips, mouth.

Tisha floats in coma world while people visit her in this one—mom, grandmother, Leo, Fat Adam, Chad, Becky, me. Zen G and Tristan have season tickets.

Summer is perennial no-show.

I sit by bed of what used to be Tisha. "How's it going?" I ask. Stupid to talk, probably. But who knows?

Engie's right. Tisha's eyelids flutter. Like she heard me?

"Be glad you're not being treated by this sadistic sack of Schlitz down in the ER, Dr. Davis," I tell her. "Remember that name. If he ever comes near you, code. Believe me, you'll be glad you did."

Hey, if you can't run black crow humor on semi-comatose burn victim, where can you run it?

"Hey, I remember you said you like to surf," I go on. "When you get better, let's go surfing together. I just learned. Tristan taught me and he's—"

Her eyes flutter, flutter, flutter.

I'm up. "Tisha? Tisha?"

Flutter closed. Damn.

I admit it. I'm acting. Read: I'm royally pissed at her. No one made her drink and drive. Hurt so many people. Kill her best friend. Wreck her own life.

Plus. I didn't even like her in the first place.

But. I judged, found her wanting. Stuck her into a little box. Laughed at her.

Tristan was right.

Now I'm trying to right my wrong.

" 'S'funny, Tisha. We have a lot in common. Like, I get all weird around a guy I like too much, too. You get wasted, I get mean. Why do we do that? It sucks to be so needy."

Her finger moves. I'm sure of it.

"Tisha? Did you move a finger? I mean, on purpose? If you can hear me, move it again. Now."

Focus. Everything. On her right hand. Will it to move. Move.

Move!

Nothing.

Schlitz. Come on. One stupid miracle. One. So I know it's possible. So I can believe—

"Zoey?"

Him.

"I thought she moved her fingers," I explain.

"Maybe."

A whisper. "No."

"Zee, about—" He stops. Starts again. "This morning I just—"

I wait. Nothing.

I get up. "So glad we had this little chat. And I know how you prefer me to leave when you arrive, so—"

He reaches for me. Gently. Hands on my arm. Zee girl meltdown.

"I'm sorry. That's what I'm trying to say. I'm so, so sorry."

For kissing me, he must mean. For leading me to think we were—could be—something we aren't. Never will be.

This is the pain that never ends,
It just goes on and on my friend . . .

"Forget it," I say. "I'm gone."

He stops me. The softest of touches, his hand on my cheek. "You don't understand."

"What?"

"I—"

"Hey, guys," Engie tells us. "Allie Drew's parents are here. To see Tisha."

The girl who killed their daughter.

Yet I shunt that drama aside. All I think about is him. His hand still on me.

What don't I understand, Tristan?

From Engie, "Uh, Guys?"

He pulls away first.

God, I wish it had been me.

13

TRISTAN

There are a few other neurological presentations nearly as odd as Tourette's. One is called Alien Hand Syndrome. The AHS patient's brain tells its hand to do something utterly normal, like pick up a pen.

But instead of picking up the pen, the hand makes an effort to strangle its owner. Or punch the patient's own face.

What don't I understand, Tristan?

When I look into Zee's haunted eyes, I hear that.

I wish transient Alien Hand Syndrome upon myself. I'd punch my lights out. Beat me bloody. And I still couldn't call it even.

I can reel off encyclopedic medical minutiae. But when it comes to Zoey, I am rendered stupid.

I don't want to feel . . . this. Whatever this is.

Yesterday, no waves. So I swam until I couldn't see my own hand in front of my face. All the time I'm out there I'm longing for—

What?

Monster waves, monster snowstorms, monster herds of caribou to shoot, monster anythings.

Anything, but this.

When I finally stagger back onto the darkened beach, there sits Greg, a lighter held under his chin illuminating his face. Like a ghoul in the night.

Last ghoul I want to see.

Over and over, he beats himself up for what happened. Doesn't want to cry on Zoey's shoulder, he tells me. He cares about her too much to put that on her. He hopes she cares about him, too.

He says: "Cuz without that—the hope of that—I can't take the real world anymore. Know what I mean?"

I do. But why tell me? Not me, for God's sake.

I saw how she kissed him at Aesop's, the night I was there with Summer. Zee Girl is not Summer, wouldn't kiss him like that unless she meant it.

But the very next night, at the Bomb, all I could think about was getting to Aesop's. To be with her. And for what? It's not like I love her. Whatever that word means.

I sit there with Greg for a long time, hearing confession.

He has no idea he's confessing to the real perp.

So yeah, I'm up for a little Alien Hand Syndrome.

Which, of course, will not strike me. Only those who are innocent. Jerome with bone cancer. Bishop with Tourette's *and* he's HIV positive. Tia. Allie.

Allie's parents materialize outside the Burn ICU. Dad bald, stooped. Or maybe that's new, from grief so heavy he can't quite hold himself upright anymore. Momma wren. Small and colorless.

The silly circles of clownish blush she's applied can't disguise the wonderful cheekbones she doesn't realize, maybe never realized, she possesses.

She clutches his arm. They walk toward us.

"Hello. I'm Arlene Drew, this is my husband, Frank."

Zoey and I introduce ourselves.

"You must be friends of Tisha's," she surmises. "Did you know my Allie, too?"

Words uttered so hopefully. What is unspoken is how much it would mean to her if we knew her daughter.

Before I can speak, Zoey says, "Yes, of course we knew Allie. She was such a lovely person, Mrs. Drew, Mr. Drew. We're so sorry for your loss."

His eyes fill. He nods, wordless.

Mrs. Drew fiddles with her vinyl purse. "I keep thinking, I need to call those nice people at the Rotary who gave Allie that scholarship to art school. They can give it to someone else. I just keep forgetting to call them."

I listen intently, as does Zoey.

Like we know what the hell she's talking about.

"We've been praying for Tisha," the woman goes on. "How is she?"

Zoey covers her incredulity, but not from me, at this woman praying for the person who killed her daughter.

"Better," I say. "But still critical."

Mrs. Drew nods. "Tisha loved Allie like a sister. We grieve for her. Frank and I know this was just a terrible accident."

Zoey can't help herself. "But Tisha was driving *drunk*. I'm sorry, Mr. and Mrs. Drew, but no one made her do that."

"I'm sure she didn't realize," Mrs. Drew insists. "Allie didn't, either. It was a mistake. I forgive Tisha."

Her husband turns away.

"Well, I guess we'll be going in now," she continues. "I hope you two are planning to come to the funeral tomorrow?"

I nod. "So many people loved Allie, Mrs. Drew. We'll all be there."

Her face grows softer. "Thank you." She fiddles with the handle of her purse. "It won't be an open casket. Allie had such a beautiful face. And what with the burns . . . We had her high school graduation picture blown up to put on the altar. That's better, don't you think?"

"Much."

"Thank you. For being so nice." Mrs. Drew kisses me, then Zoey, on the cheek. Mr. Drew shakes our hands.

They leave to go inside Tisha's room. We stand there.

Much too young to feel this damned old.

e-mail

To: Stevedaman@aol.com
From: tristmarch@juno.com
Re: Your crappy taste in music

Stevie—

You heard about the midnight rambler. It's nearly one in the morning, that damned Stones tune keeps playing in someone's room, and I don't even like it. Your fault forcing them down my throat for so many years. Greatest band of all time my ass, Stevie. You know I never get insomnia. Well, never say never. Which is why I'm tap-tap-tapping away in the dark while Chad snores across the room.

Only a few hours till morning, and the funeral I e-mailed you about. Yeah, another one. Yeah, I know just what you think of that little custom. But her parents need to do this. So we gotta do it for them.

Sounds crazy, but I wish I'd known Allie Drew better. I wouldn't feel like such a hypocrite. Her mom said she had won an art scholarship. I wish I'd known. Asked her about it. Listened to her dreams. I was too busy trying to dodge her bud. Coma girl.

You asked about Summer. I was with her tonight. Walked on the beach. Rolled in the dunes. Great sex is as close to death as you can get, buddy. I was there. So was she. Afterward, she was turned inside out for a little while. Let me see the seams. Held me close. Asked where I'd been the past couple of nights.

The truth I didn't tell her. But I will tell you. I was with Victoria Seng. Dr. Vic to us lowly SCRUBS. She's unhinged from her sister's death. I found her on the roof of the hospital, poised over the edge of the wall, arms in take-off position. Maybe she would have jumped, maybe not. I'll never know. I went home with her. Held her all night. She didn't cry. Didn't speak. Just breathed. The next night, same thing.

In the morning she told me she was taking a leave of absence from the hospital. Thanked me. Then I left.

I will not tell Summer that. Or anyone. But you.

Summer, I gave some half-assed story to. But in any event, ten minutes later, no longer inside out, she happily went her way, I went mine. That's why she's the one, Stevie. She's sexual perfection. She doesn't ask from me what I don't have to give. So what if I still see Zoey's face in my dreams? Her heart is a lonely hunter.

No, I didn't call Billie yet, so shut up about it. Better yet, get on a damned plane and tell me to my face how pissed off you are. I don't care how bad your voice sounds now, either. I always was the only one crazy enough to understand you anyway. 'Cuz I really need to see you, Stevie. Bad. I'm drowning here. I think maybe only a big bald surfer with soon-to-be banished brain cancer can save me.

Now, The Doors. *There* was a band.

Love,
Trist

14

ZOEY

"Zoey? Zoey? Help me, please! Get me out, please!"

"Where are you, Mom? I can't see you!"

"Over here. Look over here. Please, save me, please!"

I'm tearing, tearing through the rubble of the Murrah Building, my fingernails ripping off on shattered concrete, but I can't find my mother, her voice gets weaker, I have to reach her, but I can't breathe just like she can't breathe, but I have to because I have to save her have to—

"The car! Watch out!"

"What car, Mom?"

"On fire! Fire!"

I laugh crazily. " 'Cuz she smokes, Mom. That's all. She smokes so much that—"

"Help me!"

"She can wiggle her fingers, Mom. Watch!"

Gasping, I sit up. Eyes blink in the dark. Drink in air. Arrhythmias tattoo my chest wall.

Breathe in, out. In, out. This is how you stay alive.

Sometimes I can sleep again, the nightmare gone.

Sometimes I can't. Walk the dunes. Stare at the monsters in my head. Dawn always comes. Eventually.

Only this time, something is different. Something cold on my neck. Wrong. Something very wrong.

I dread going back, but.

I rewind the nightmare. My mom, like always. I can't get to her, like always. And then, different.

A car. On fire. My torn fingernails.

Because she smokes so much, I say.

Holy Schlitz.

No, it can't be.

For a long time coming, I debate self in darkest hours just before the dawn. FP and Becky sleep. Debate reaches stalemate. I have but one choice.

Go to Effing-Huh and prove self right. Or wrong.

I dress silently. Little cat's feet it into bathroom. Snag something, stick it into pocket. Ease out of unsweet.

I hit chill predawn air. And Tristan. Sitting on the curb. No surfboard. No wet suit. Just him.

He turns, sees me. For a moment his face goes joyful.

But no. Must be my imagination. Trick of half-light. Product of insanity that has me doing insane thing I'm about to do.

"The sun also rises, Zee girl," he tells me. "Why do you think that is?"

"Physics. The Earth rotates."

He laughs. "Yeah. No prime mover spiritual renewal crap for you. Heading for the beach?"

"No." Then out pops, "Look, this is insane, but . . . please come with me."

He's up, an implicit yes. "Where?"

At Effing-Huh, we flash badges, slip past Big Nurse into Burn ICU. Bright lights. Monitors beep. Patient seems unchanged.

"Tisha?" I whisper. Then louder. "Tisha!"

Zip. Tristan says nothing. I offer idiotic half-smile for no reason.

Note to self: report ASAP to psych pavilion for full psychiatric work-up and possible medication.

"Tisha?" Nothing.

So. I lean toward her right hand. Which yesterday fluttered at me. Scorched fingernails peek out of bandages.

Scorched pink.

Tisha was unmanicured. I remember when Tristan took her hand.

I feel sick. Beyond sick.

Allie's funeral is in three hours.

"This isn't Tisha," I tell Tristan.

"What?"

New note to self: try to keep psychotic break private until after rehab.

Too late now.

I explain what I think. What I know.

"You think this is Allie?" he asks me.

I nod.

Tristan comes close. Looks at one hand. The other.

"You held hands with Tisha, Tristan," I remind him. "Don't you remember her nails were bare?"

He hesitates. "Allie's parents identified their daughter."

"Burned beyond recognition."

"Zee, Allie doesn't drink. She told me so herself, when I made sure she had—" He stops.

"Tisha's car keys," he finishes.

Ice on my neck again.

From the looks of Tristan, his, too.

Allie had Tisha's car keys.

We stare at each other. An impasse.

"Feels like a really bad TV show," I note.

"That would take in all TV shows," he notes.

"Okay, Sleuthboy," I say. "Tisha said at Aesop's she was horribly allergic to Summer's perfume. Gives her hives. De Rien."

I pull it from out of my pocket.

"You might consider switching from medicine to a life of crime."

"Hey, what the hell do you think you're doing in here?" a voice booms.

Big Butt Big Nurse stands there. Reeks of supervisory position. Beyond pissed.

"Visiting," I say. "We're SCRUBS." Badges flash.

"I don't care if you're Sonny and Cher reincarnated, you're outta here."

Tristan focuses on her, talks his talk. As fullfledged insanity hits me, I spray person in bed's fingertips with De Rien. Knock-off De Rein, actually. But still.

Tristan gets Big Butt Big Nurse talking about her big-ass beagle. The vet says big-ass beagle needs to lose weight.

"Barney on a diet," she scoffs. "Stupidest thing I ever heard."

Right. I'm nodding. I'm turning around.

"Next thing, he'll say Barney needs to do Pilates, or—"

I genuflect to look at pink-tinged brown-singed nails.

"Put my hamster on Jenny Craig."

Bumpless. No hives.

I nudge Tristan.

He looks.

No hives.

"Holy Mother Mary!" Big Butt Big Nurse calls.

What brought on her religious fervor, I don't know.

But then I do.

Inspection of hives-free fingers surpassed notice of hives-free eyes.

Which are now open.

Fixed on me.

"Praise God. I'm calling the doctors." Big Butt Big Nurse pushes every alarm button in sight.

"If you can hear me, blink once," Tristan says.

Eyes blink once.

"Dr. Ransom, Dr. Charles Ransom, to the Burn ICU," Big Butt Nurse announces over the loud hailer. "Dr. Charles Ransom, Burn ICU."

Tristan shines his special smile on whoever is in the bed. "Welcome back," he says.

Moment of truth. My eyes meet Tristan's. Somehow, my hand is in his.

"Dr. Ransom, Dr. Charles Ransom, Burn ICU."

The loud hailer echoes.

I say, "This probably sounds crazy, but we're not sure who you are."

"It's okay." Tristan nods reassuringly. "Can you talk?"

Nothing.

"What we need you to do," I say slowly, raising my voice over the alarms, "is blink once for yes, and twice for no. Can you do that?"

One blink from the girl.

"Great," Tristan tells her.

"Do you know who you are?"

One blink.

I fill my lungs with air. Squeeze Tristan's fingers in mine.

And I ask, "Is your name Tisha Henry?"

Before she can blink, a squadron of doctors, led by Dr. Charles Ransom, bursts into the ICU.

CHERIE BENNETT and JEFF GOTTESFELD

Cherie Bennett and her husband, Jeff Gottesfeld, often write on teen themes. This novel is their latest for Berkley; they wrote the *Trash* series together, while Cherie authored the best-selling Berkley series *Sunset Island*. Cherie writes both paperback and hardcover fiction—*Life in the Fat Lane*, *Zink*—while her Copley News Service syndicated column, "Hey Cherie!" appears in papers coast to coast. She is also one of America's finest young playwrights and a back-to-back winner of The Kennedy Center's "New Visions/New Voices" playwriting award. Cherie and Jeff live in Nashville and Los Angeles, and may always be contacted at P.O. Box 150326, Nashville, TN 37215; e-mail to authorchik@aol.com

TRASH

Welcome to *Trash*, the hippest, raciest TV talk show in history. Ten thousand teens apply and six are picked as interns, with an awesome apartment thrown in. The best summer ever, right? Maybe!

For Chelsea, life at *Trash* is a total sleaze-fest. Not only are the hours long, but she also gets to scoop up after her boss's dalmatians!

Thank goodness for the other interns—two great girl roommates and three gorgeous guys. Fantastic friends, hot romance, a summer to remember...so long as no one—especially—unearths Chelsea's grim dark secret.

All books by Cherie Bennett & Jeff Gottesfeld
FROM THE BESTSELLING AUTHOR OF *SUNSET ISLAND*: